Jocelyn deserved to know how she wasted her adoration. He was broken and finally admitted it to her out loud.

Maybe saying it aloud—*I have PTSD*—would help make the condition go away.

If only it were that easy.

"You sure you want me to help with that fundraiser? A balloon may pop and I might freak out on you or something."

From nowhere her cool hands caressed his cheeks. Jocelyn went up on her toes to buss his lips, catching him by surprise.

"Yes," she said, gazing into his face. "I still want you to help me with the fundraiser." There was a playful glint in her coffee-bean-colored eyes. "I also hope you'll reconsider about reenlisting." With her hands still framing his face, her lashes fluttered downward then back up.

Their gazes met and held in an I-refuse-to-be-the-first-to-look-away contest. He could hear her breathe, and there was that sweet flower bloom and vanilla shampoo scent again….

Dear Reader,

I'm so happy to share Lucas Grady's story with you. He is Anne Grady's younger brother from my debut Special Edition (March 2012), *Courting His Favorite Nurse*.

Lucas is a good man who has served his country but who has come home with some extra baggage on board. Good thing there's a girl next door named Jocelyn, who sees more in him than he sees in himself.

I don't know about you, but I love friends-to-lovers stories because they can get so complicated—*hey, what are these new feelings I have for you? You used to be that pest next door. Now, well, you look pretty darn great!* Throw in some obstacles like PTSD for one, an abusive ex-boyfriend for another, plus a meddling—with good intentions—family, and watch the fireworks explode.

Regarding post-traumatic stress disorder, I hope I have honored in this book the uphill struggles of those affected by PTSD. I know each person's journey is different, and I tried to be realistic yet upbeat in the telling of *The Medic's Homecoming*.

So come along with me, welcome back to Whispering Oaks, get reacquainted with the Grady clan, especially Lucas, and meet that girl next door, Jocelyn.

I love to hear from readers at www.lynnemarshall.com, where you can sign up for my weekly blog, and an occasional newsletter. Come say hello on Facebook and friend me at www.facebook.com/LynneMarshall.Page.

Happy reading!

Lynne

THE MEDIC'S HOMECOMING

LYNNE MARSHALL

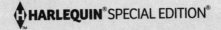

Recycling programs
for this product may
not exist in your area.

ISBN-13: 978-0-373-65756-8

THE MEDIC'S HOMECOMING

Copyright © 2013 by Janet Maarschalk

Printed in U.S.A.

Books by Lynne Marshall

Harlequin Special Edition

Courting His Favorite Nurse #2178
The Medic's Homecoming #2274

Harlequin Medical Romance

Her Baby's Secret Father
Her L.A. Knight
In His Angel's Arms
Single Dad, Nurse Bride
Pregnant Nurse, New-Found Family
Assignment: Baby
Temporary Doctor, Surprise Father
The Boss and Nurse Albright
The Heart Doctor and the Baby
The Christmas Baby Bump

Other titles by this author available in ebook format.

LYNNE MARSHALL

Lynne used to worry that she had a serious problem with daydreaming—then she discovered she was supposed to write those stories! A late bloomer, Lynne came to fiction writing after her children were nearly grown. Now she battles the empty nest by writing stories that always include a romance, sometimes medicine, a dose of mirth, or both, but always stories from her heart. She is a Southern California native, a dog lover, a cat admirer, a power walker and avid reader.

This book is dedicated to the men and women
who must deal with PTSD every day.

Also, special thanks to my son, J.P., for loaning me
his tattoos for this book. Love you.

Chapter One

Lucas couldn't sleep. What else was new? He thought maybe things would be different once he got home, but no.

He threw back the covers and slid into the leather flip-flops he'd picked up at the base PX, then headed out back to the garage and his 1965 Mustang. The classic car he'd saved up for with part-time jobs—bought long before he was old enough to drive and mostly rebuilt before he'd left home at eighteen—seemed to call out to him.

As the cool night wind pushed him along, he glanced next door, finding a light on in the upstairs bedroom. The same room he'd tossed pebbles at the night before he left for boot camp. Jocelyn hadn't opened the window then, so he'd never gotten to say goodbye. Damn, had that been ten years ago?

He flipped on the light at the garage side entrance, but nothing happened. Fumbling around in the dark he bumped into his car and reached above, swinging his hand back and forth until he found the dangling chain then yanked. A single bulb dimly lit the garage. Rolling back the thick plastic car-cover, he took a deep inhale. Grease and oil perked up his senses. This was home. The garage and the peace it had always offered. His classic car.

How could his father call him a slacker when he'd never worked harder on anything in his life?

Glancing around the countertops, he found a rag and walked the perimeter of the Mustang, wiping away the dust on the chipped and flaking paint, the smoother areas covered in sprayed-on primer. He took his time, reacquainting himself with the sleek body and chrome.

He'd flown into LAX from North Carolina earlier that evening, greeted by his sister, Anne, and her boyfriend, Jack. They delivered him home to the Grady idea of a hero's welcome—Mom's famous yellow cake with buttercream chocolate frosting. Still one of the best desserts he'd ever had.

Lucas looked at the beat-up Harley in the corner of the garage. Though in their mid-fifties, Mom and Dad still enjoyed their weekend rides. Well, they used to, anyway—before the accident.

It had been a little shocking to find his father in a wheelchair, his right leg and opposite arm in casts. Still an imposing figure at six feet four inches—though you couldn't tell in that wheelchair—Kieran Grady hadn't changed much. His sandy blond hair had been invaded by silver, mostly around the temples, and he looked craggier than Lucas remembered. Probably from all the years of coaching in the California sun catching up with him. His steel-blue stare, though, was unchanged, and he'd used those inquiring eyes to thoroughly check out Lucas tonight. Did Dad have a clue what Lucas had been through in the desert?

No one could, unless they'd witnessed it themselves.

Mom, other than going the bottle-brown route with her hair, had looked basically the same. She wore her signature casual jeans, though now they'd been traded in for designer jeans with shiny studs along the pockets and stitched flowers at the flared legs. Still preferring flashy patterned tops, her bright pink cast competed with the loud colors. Her welcoming smile and the tears welling in her eyes told him all he needed to know—she was happy to have him home, no matter the circumstances.

As Lucas thought about that night, the tugging in his chest let him know it was good to see his parents again. Both of them.

While he tinkered with the car, Lucas geared up for the next couple of weeks being his father's medical attendant. It would be tough but a damn sight easier than performing medic duties in the desert.

He stood back and stared at his Mustang, then

scanned the family garage, littered with boxes stored in the rafters. So many memories.

Was it good to be home?

"Hey," his sister Anne said from the door.

He controlled his surprise, trained his eyes on her and kept rubbing the car. "I can't believe Dad kept this around."

"I think he knew you'd come after him if he ever tried to sell it."

Man, the tension between him and his dad had made the welcome-home yellow cake with chocolate buttercream frosting go down like cardboard. Would Dad ever forgive him for enlisting? It was Dad's dream to send him to college, just like Anne and Lark, but Lucas hadn't wanted to go to college. He wasn't one for hitting the books like his sisters. No, he preferred the basics: getting his hands dirty and fixing things. Come to think of it, being a medic in the field had a lot to do with fixing things, like gaping body injuries, burned skin and gunshot wounds. Books and papers, well, he didn't have the patience for that stuff.

When he'd tested out for medic over engineer on the military aptitude battery, he'd almost demanded a retest. That was *Anne's* dream, to be a doctor—though she'd become a nurse—and these days baby sister Lark was the one back east in medical school.

"What are you doing up?" she asked.

"Can't sleep."

"Too much excitement?"

His smile felt more like a grimace. "Yeah, maybe that's it."

The worst part of his post-traumatic stress disorder was dealing with insomnia. He couldn't remember the last time he'd slept more than a couple hours. When he did manage to fall asleep, he'd wake with a start, heart pounding up his throat, every muscle tensed, prepared to fight for his life. Or his sleep would be restless with fits and jerks like he was still fighting the war. He'd wake up more exhausted than when he'd gone to bed.

What he'd give for one good night's sleep....

Because he was exhausted most of the time, he snapped at people, which wouldn't go over well with his dad. Only his buddies in the field understood. How would he adjust to being back to civilian life, where no one else did?

"Can I bring you anything from the kitchen?" Of the three siblings, Anne looked the most like their mother, and she'd barely changed since the last time he'd seen her—Christmas three years ago. Her light brown hair was different, cut just above her shoulders now instead of halfway down her back. She'd borne the brunt of caring for Mom and Dad the past few weeks, and it showed in dark inverted arcs under her eyes. Or maybe it was just the dingy garage lighting. She probably thought he looked like hell, too.

Something else was going on with her, but he didn't have a clue. He'd picked up on that "something" between her and Jack on the drive home from the airport tonight, but he couldn't get a handle on what it might be.

"I'm fine, Anne, thanks." Hell, she'd always been able to read his moods, and his go-away-and-leave-me-alone approach wouldn't keep her off his scent for long. She'd probably noticed him flinch when he dove into the backseat of the car at the airport at the same time a car backfired. "What are you doing up?" he said.

"I saw the light and just wanted to check and make sure everything was okay."

"Hope I didn't wake you."

"Nah, I was awake, anyway. I'm going back inside now," she said.

"I'm okay, Anne." He glanced to make sure she wasn't worried about him. He couldn't read her sleepy-looking brown eyes. "See you in the morning."

She hesitated, looking more alert and glancing a bit longer than necessary, probably using her uncanny, sister fib-o-meter to size him up, then she nodded. "Night."

To her, when they were growing up, he'd always been the goofball kid brother. He'd given her plenty of reasons for that, with all his shenanigans and poorly thought-out schemes. How many times had he gotten caught and in trouble for his less-than-bright ideas? Anne had often come to his aid and stuck up for him. He fought a smile, glimpsing a portion of his face in the car's cracked rearview mirror.

She'd tried, though. She'd tricked him into signing up for the track team by telling him it would get him out of those dreaded physical fitness tests. And he quit smoking after she showed him horrifying pictures of cancerous lungs from her high school anatomy class.

Lucas could have been a huge screwup if it weren't for Anne. When she used to call him out for being a jerk, it'd felt like a stab through the heart, but she always managed to get through to him. She didn't buy his bad-boy act for a second, even if everyone else did. And that was fine by him. Truth was, he liked it better when he made her and Mom laugh, not worry. He rubbed his chest thinking how long Mom had been worrying about him. Ten years, counting basic training. The last thing Mom needed to know was he'd cut his PTSD treatment short to come home and take care of her and Dad.

Once Anne was gone, he switched on the old radio in the corner and listened to static oldies through the tinny speaker. When he'd finished wiping down the car, he sat inside and cleaned the tattered leather upholstery and faded dashboard, fingered the steering wheel and imagined driving with the top down, feeling the winds of Whispering Oaks rushing through his hair. Now that he had some hair. What was that word, or more importantly, that feeling, he'd forgotten? Carefree.

He let out a breath. The last time he'd felt carefree was around the time his biggest charge was pulling little Jocelyn Howard's braids and having her chase him around the yard. But once he'd hit puberty, that was child's play.

With the late hour, the static was coarse on the radio. He got out of the car to turn it off and to try for a couple hours of sleep. On his way inside, he noticed the light was out in Jocelyn's bedroom. He thought about looking for some pebbles to toss at her window, just to bug her, but he was only wearing his army-issue brown boxers. What kind of impression would that make? Besides, if this time she opened the window, he wouldn't have a clue what to say.

Mere hours later, a loud knock on the door woke Lucas. "I'll be right there," he said, husky-voiced. He hopped to attention, threw on some shorts and a crew-neck T-shirt and fumbled for the knob. The last thing he needed was for Dad to see the tattoos on his shoulders. Pushing open the door, he saw Anne through bleary eyes.

"We need your help," she said.

"That's what I'm here for." He strode across the hall to his parents' room, pretending to be awake, as Anne's cell phone rang.

"Go ahead," he said. "Answer it. I'll take care of this." He continued into the bedroom as she back-stepped down the hallway, already talking.

"Well, good morning, bright eyes!" his father said, obviously trying to get a rise out of him. How many times growing up had Lucas heard that phrase when he hadn't looked alert enough at the breakfast table?

"Hey, Dad. So how do we do this?" he said, scratching his chest, determined not to knee-jerk a snotty re-sponse to his father's jab.

Kieran sat at the edge of the bed, hair ruffled, eyes grumpy, sheets twisted and knotted around him.

Lucas let a slow smile tug at one corner of his mouth.

"You know, you're not looking so bright-eyed your-self, Dad."

"It's been hell, Lucas. These damn casts are driving me nuts. I'm counting the days until they'll take them off."

Nearby, Bart, his parents' replacement for the kids, warily eyed Lucas. Lucas approached, ignoring the Rhodesian ridgeback's low growl. "Good boy," he said. Though big and imposing-looking, the dog's real personality was betrayed by a wagging long brown tail.

Soon, the huge dog licked Lucas's arm as if they'd been friends forever.

Only sheer will could have gotten Dad to sit up on his own because Mom, who stood close by with a yellow robe over her shoulders and that bright pink cast, couldn't possibly have helped him with her one good hand. The man was too damn big. Good thing Dad had a will of steel.

"What did you always say to me, 'This too shall pass,' or something?" Lucas said, wanting to ease his dad's frazzled mood.

Kieran grimaced. "Using my own words against me—that's cold, son." He flashed a brief grin at Lucas—more of a *touché* than an affirmation. *Truce. For now.*

"Let me explain how we do this," his mom, Beverly, said, stepping around the bed to her husband's side.

He'd done thousands of patient transfers in his nine years of active duty. But Lucas bit his tongue and let her explain their routine for getting Dad into the wheelchair.

Forty-five minutes later he'd helped his father wash and get dressed and had rolled him into the kitchen for breakfast. After years of helping his share of proud-but-wounded soldiers in the field, Lucas understood how humiliating it was for a grown man to need someone else to help him bathe. So he'd offered his dad all due respect, looking away when necessary, and the man had appreciated it.

He could tell because Dad had let his guard down a little. They carried on a civilized conversation…as if new acquaintances. Same stuff he'd covered with Anne on the drive from the airport. Weather, food, old friends. Though the conversation with his dad had felt stilted, anything was better than snarky attacks.

At least his dad hadn't mentioned his appearance. Lucas had caught a glimpse of himself in the bathroom with Dad and had to laugh at how bad he looked. He'd at least managed to throw some water on his face and run damp fingers through his hair. He'd thought about shaving when he'd shaved his father but decided to wait until later when he showered. And Dad would have nothing to do with the soul patch he'd tried to talk him into, opting for a clean shave. He noted that Dad's hairline seemed to be getting higher and higher.

In the kitchen, after gulping down the orange juice Anne had set on the counter for him, Lucas headed out front for the newspaper. The neighborhood hadn't changed a bit—a meandering street lined with pine and ash trees, mostly single-story ranch houses except for the Howards' next door and a few others. The beige of the Grady home was accented with red brick, which set it apart from the otherwise similar homes along the street. Bushes or rustic wood fences divided most property lines.

He glanced up and down the block as he searched for the paper on yet another sunny day in Southern California. God, he'd missed that. The paper had been thrown between the family car in the driveway and the long row of box bushes bordering the Howards' yard. As he bent to reach for it, he heard footfalls running down the sidewalk. He popped his head over the car bumper in time to see Jocelyn jog by. He hadn't seen her in almost ten years, yet he instantly recognized her.

She wore black thigh-length form-fitting running shorts and a sports bra. More athletic than voluptuous, she could get away with it. And did she ever. Her long torso, thin legs and arms looked fit, covered in a light bronze California tan. Her fawn-colored hair, held high in a ponytail over the back of her visor, shone in the sun.

Flooded with good memories and hit by an impulse, he shot out from behind the car after her. Her long ponytail wagged back and forth with each stride, begging to be yanked. Nearly catching up with her, he reached out for her hair and tugged.

"Hey there," he said.

She gasped and spun around, recoiled with muscles tensed, eyes large and dark with surprise—or possibly fear. *Idiot, you scared her!* Maybe he should have thought through his bright idea a bit more.

Just as suddenly, she beamed with recognition.

* * *

With the yank on her hair, Jocelyn almost leaped out of her skin. Every muscle in her body went on alert as memories of another time she hadn't been paying close enough attention to coursed through her. She spun around…and couldn't believe her eyes. Trying to catch her breath and reel in her wildly beating heart, she broke into a smile.

It was Lucas, all six feet and change of him. He stood before her wearing a T-shirt and shorts that seemed to have been left in the dryer too long. He looked like a never-forgotten, though rumpled, dream. A dream from ten years ago that hadn't ever faded.

She grinned wider, her lower lip trembling. His shoulders seemed broader, and his flat stomach, muscled arms and legs advertised one super-fit male. His dark brown hair stuck out in several different directions, and by the goofy, upside-down attempt at a smile he was glad to see her.

After ten years, Lucas had finally come home, and the sight of him practically made her knees buckle.

"Lucas!"

Chapter Two

Jocelyn kicked out at Lucas. "I could crown you!" she said, taking a swing at him. "You could have given me a heart attack."

He dodged her swing. "I'm sorry." He held up his hands, fighting back his grin and enjoying every second of her protest. "I saw you run by, and, well, I never could resist pulling your ponytail." The warm feeling in his chest caught him off guard, plus the fact he was genuinely glad to see her.

"Were you hiding in the bushes or something?"

He tapped the newspaper in the air. "I'm not that messed up. I was getting the paper."

Color rose on her olive-toned cheeks.

"Who says you're messed up? You're just a freak

who likes to sneak up on unsuspecting women and pull their hair." She squared off, hands on her hips, and stared at him.

"Not true. Not women. Only one unsuspecting woman. You." He folded his arms and watched.

Man, she'd changed, yet she hadn't. Gotten a lot taller—almost as tall as him. Filled out a little. Grew some hips. Looked good in sports gear. Had the same pretty teeth and shiny brown eyes…and he hadn't even washed his face yet. What the hell was he thinking?

"So, you're home for good now?"

"Yup. Got back last night."

"Fantastic. Welcome home." There was that pretty and contagious grin again. He felt dumb smiling this much so early in the morning, but, there you go, he was. "Then I guess I'll see you around," she said.

He nodded, wondering why he'd bothered to bug her. What was the point?

"Great!" She turned, tossing her ponytail, and resumed running. His gaze followed her long, smooth strides for a few seconds.

Without looking back she lifted her arm and waved, as if she knew he was still there. Watching.

For a moment, he'd felt like that kid he used to be, the one full of bravado, pretending to take on the universe, not like the world-weary dude he'd turned into.

"I'm glad you're home, Lucas," she called out two house-lengths away.

He cupped his hands around his mouth. "You run like a girl."

She gave a single-finger salute and picked up her stride. It made him laugh, and he couldn't remember the last time he'd laughed.

You know what? Maybe he *was* glad to be home.

Monday afternoon, after performing all of the basic duties for his father and setting him free in the wheelchair, he'd caught his sister making plane reservations to return home on Saturday. It only made sense. She worked as an RN in Oregon and couldn't stay forever. But was he ready to take on the whole show—to be nursemaid, chauffeur, cook and delivery boy?

Lucas wandered out to the garage with his new best friend, Bart, hot on his trail. Well, best friend since he'd shared some of his peanut butter sandwich with him at lunch. Lost in tinkering with his Mustang, he'd enjoy the solitude for what few days were left before Anne went home. Time flew by, and soon it was late afternoon and he heard Anne scraping the grill and firing up the barbecue.

"Annie-belle, could you throw another shrimp on the barbie?" Kieran, using his worst Australian accent, sounded really close. Lucas shook his head. He had to hand it to his father—he never gave up. And somehow he had gotten the wheelchair out to the garage all by himself. "I've invited Jocelyn for dinner."

Jocelyn?

Lucas pretended he hadn't heard. Fortunately, since being cooped up in the house the past month, Dad had the attention span of someone with ADD hopped up on caffeine. Kieran's melancholy gaze had already drifted to the totaled Harley motorcycle parked in the corner of the garage.

"It's a crying shame, isn't it?" Kieran said.

"Most definitely."

"Too bad your specialty isn't motorcycles instead of Mustangs."

"I used to know a guy named David in auto shop who loved bikes. Want me to look him up for you?"

"Your mother would divorce me if I ever got back on one of those babies."

"You've got a point."

"Hey, let me run something by you," Kieran said, shifting to yet another topic as he rolled his motorized wheelchair into the garage.

"I want you to help out Jocelyn with our annual athletic department fund-raiser."

"Dad, I'm really not interested in…"

"I need you to help me, Lucas. I can do all the phoning and can make contacts with vendors and solicit donations, but I need you to be my legs." Dad looked earnest, the corners of his blue eyes crinkled and staring Lucas down. "Jocelyn's great. But the thing is, she doesn't think she can sub for me as coach because she lost her track scholarship when she was at the university and she's insecure. She needs help with the fund-raiser and track. And that's where I need to throw her a crumb—you. Not that you're a crumb."

This was the first Lucas had heard about Jocelyn bombing out of her scholarship. Hmm. She bombed out.

He slacked. Maybe he and Jocelyn had more in common than he ever thought.

"This is our big fund-raiser for the entire year. I need someone to watch over Jocelyn, help her out and report back to me. Someone to be my eyes and ears until I can be there myself."

"Your snoop, you mean."

"That's just an added bonus." Kieran looked serious. "I really need your help. She needs your help. The Whispering Oaks track team needs your help. I'm not sure I'm ever going to be able to be head coach again, and this team has lots of potential."

"I feel so special." Lucas put splayed fingers over his chest.

The old man was laying it on pretty thick. Despite himself, Lucas listened with great interest, wondering how he'd let himself get sucked into the plan. Oh, right. He was the coach's son.

As he listened to his dad, Lucas stuck the key into the ignition of the Mustang, turned it and after a few rum-rum-rums, a tingle of excitement bled out from his chest as the engine almost turned over before moaning like a distressed horse.

"I thought you already jumped the battery with my cables," Kieran said.

"I did one better. I bought a new one," Lucas said. "It started okay earlier. Maybe it's the alternator." If he turned out to be right about the alternator, as soon as he cashed his last check he'd buy a new one, which was no easy feat when dealing with classic cars. He'd have to get online tonight and research a few possibilities. Good thing he'd saved up substantially during his army stint because the car could suck him dry. In the meantime, he'd have to wait to take his baby for a test-drive.

Lucas shut the hood and wiped his hands, turning in time to see Jocelyn walk up. She wore tan cropped pants, double-layered tank tops in bright yellow and dark orange, flashy gladiator sandals and even had a pedicure complete with a tiny flower on each big toe. Nice.

"Hi, Lucas," Jocelyn said, losing her step on the gravel. She opened her arms, and he gave her a quick one-arm hug, feeling uncomfortable. Seeing her now was nothing like the other day when it was just the two of them. Anne was bound to make a big deal out of them meeting up again. His dad wanted him to help her coach. The whole situation made him tense. The last thing he needed was pressure over anything. Not in his state.

Jocelyn stepped back uncertainly. "How are you?" she asked.

"Fine. Just fine." He glanced at the ground, molars pressed tight. "I hear you're house-sitting for your parents."

"Yeah, they're finally taking that RV road trip they've always dreamed about."

"There she is," Kieran said, rolling out of the garage, Bart tugging on the knotted rope in his hand.

"You wanted to talk to me, Coach Grady?" Jocelyn

asked. To Lucas, she sounded relieved to have a purpose for being there.

Lucas chuckled. "He's got big plans for the fundraiser this year. How are you at being micromanaged?"

"I'm right here and I can hear you," Dad said, droll as ever.

In jest, Lucas flashed her a warning glance. "Let me know if you need backup."

"That's the last time I run my game plans by you," Kieran muttered, obviously unfazed by Lucas's jab, maybe even enjoying the guy banter.

"I guess I'd better see what you've got in mind." Jocelyn tossed Lucas a playful look, stepped behind the wheelchair and rolled it toward the back door, which had a makeshift ramp. She glanced over her shoulder and mouthed "thanks."

"Good luck." He raised a brow and enjoyed the color tinting her cheeks when she smiled.

"Don't listen to him, Jocelyn," Kieran said, sounding anything but perturbed.

He watched Jocelyn push his father into the house, liking the sway of her hips, then glanced up to find Anne watching him. Yeah, snoopy big sisters noticed stuff like that.

"Aren't you supposed to be barbecuing?" he said.

Once Kieran and Jocelyn were well inside the house, Anne used her playground whisper. "She is so adorable, don't you think?"

"Back off, Sis," he said, heading toward the garage.

He didn't mean to snap at Anne, but his father had

already laid out his cockamamie plan for Lucas to help with the sports department fund-raiser. He didn't need his sister playing matchmaker on top of that.

Sure, being the coach's kid, he'd attended the annual athletic event since he was little and had always enjoyed it, but never did he ever want to help plan it. Too bad Anne wasn't sticking around. That was more her thing.

He didn't appreciate the obvious matchmaking on his father's part, either. Now, with Anne's comments, he was beginning to feel the brunt of a family conspiracy. *Guess what, folks—I'm not looking for a girlfriend.*

If his dad was trying to get him some job experience by asking him to look after Jocelyn, he was barking up the wrong tree. Chasing a bunch of teen runners around the Tartan track would have about as much clout on his thin résumé as being a medic in the army would in getting a job in a hospital. Unless he went back to school, there wasn't a place in California that would hire him without a degree. Good thing he had that small nest egg saved up.

College. The last thing he felt like doing was going back to school. But it seemed like the only option at this point. Truth was, though, he didn't have a clue what he wanted to do next. He'd always planned to stick it out in the military. But then the damn PTSD started.

Now what?

"Pass the veggies, Annie-belle, would you?" Mr. Grady said, sitting at the head of the huge, white-washed, French country-style dining table. The bank of ceiling-to-wainscoting windows let in peach-tinged evening light. Gusts of wind battered and rumbled the double panes.

Even though Jocelyn had worked with him for the past eight months and known him since she was a baby, she still couldn't bring herself to call him by his first name. He'd always been Mr. Grady. Ditto for Mrs. Grady. Using her first name just didn't seem appropriate.

"Is this jasmine rice?" Mrs. Grady sniffed and closed her eyes.

Anne nodded with a hint of a proud smile. "I thought you might like that."

"I never thought you had it in you, sweetheart, but you've turned out to be a good cook," Mrs. Grady said.

"Gee, thanks, Mom." Anne's sarcasm put the cherry on top of the backhanded compliment.

For an only child like Jocelyn, a large family dinner with everyone passing food and chatting was a special treat. When she was young, longing to have brothers and sisters, she used to dream she was one of the Grady kids. When she hit preadolescence, having developed a huge crush, she was glad she *wasn't* Lucas's sister.

As the relaxed dinner banter continued, Jocelyn passed quick looks at Lucas. He'd left home ten years ago built like a long-distance runner. He'd filled out, muscled up and looked all man in a natural way. Not all men looked like that. Her ex-fiancé sure hadn't.

She needed to look away before Lucas caught her again, but, uh-oh, he'd noticed. What was that, the sixth time? She made a quick smile and took another bite of Japanese eggplant, grilled to perfection by Anne.

Speaking of perfection...Lucas had turned into a gorgeous man. His classic pentagonal-shaped face with high forehead, squared jaw and angular chin was striking to say the least. The military-short hair was filling in, darker than the brown she'd remembered. He didn't seem to care about combing it, and it stuck out in assorted directions. Tonight he'd wound up with a faux-hawk ridge on top of his head. His hazel eyes evaded contact, but she'd managed to catch his gaze a time or two or three. And he'd actually smiled for her—well, if you counted lips that turned downward instead of up while showing some teeth a smile. An upside-down smile that looked like he was in pain. Like smiling had become foreign to him.

So a smile from Lucas wasn't necessarily a happy thing. She'd have to think on that for a while.

As great as he looked, Lucas seemed withdrawn and guarded—nothing like the crazy kid and overconfident teen she used to know. Well, she wasn't nearly as carefree as she used to be, either. Life had a way of teaching everyone lessons about caution.

Kieran tapped his knife against his water glass. "So, here's the deal. Jocelyn has been taking over the Whispering Oaks track team as head coach while I've been laid up, and now Lucas has agreed to help her out with track meets and the annual sports fund-raiser."

Lucas's brows shot up. "Who said anything about

track meets? You just asked me to help out with the fund-raiser and occasional practices."

"You can't expect Jocelyn to run a meet on her own," Mr. Grady said. "She's got a couple of assistant coaches, but they'll all have their hands full. We need another body, and you make the most sense."

Lucas shook his head, took another bite of rice with vegetables and, by the way his jaw worked overtime, ground the food into pulp.

Jocelyn chewed her bottom lip, then flashed her cheerleading smile. "Mr. Grady."

"Call me Kieran, would you, please?"

"Uh, Kieran." It came out completely unnatural. "I think I can find more help. Maybe Jack…"

"Jack volunteers for the fire department on Saturdays," Anne spoke up. "He wouldn't be available for the weekend meets."

"Well, maybe he could help at the weekday practices." Jocelyn's smile was quickly fading, but she wasn't going to let Lucas get put on the spot. Not because of her own failings. Not because she was being a wuss about running the team on her own. Not because she still felt guilty about losing her track scholarship.

"Lucas, honey," Mrs. Grady said. "You used to love track. Maybe you'd enjoy sharing your experiences with the kids. And Jocelyn could use your help. Please think about it."

"Yup. Sure, Mom," he said, short, clipped words heralding the closure of the subject.

Stilted silence followed. Jocelyn's smile faded to nonexistent. *I should be able to handle things myself.* But was she even worthy of being a coach? What was the old saying: "Those who can, do; those who can't, teach"?

Lucas took a long draw of his ice water. "Well, I'm not sure what you want me to do for the fund-raiser, Jocelyn, but once Annie leaves on Saturday, I don't know how available I'll be for much of anything."

"You're leaving, Anne?" Beverly said, concern drawing her brows together.

Anne flashed a thanks-a-lot look at Lucas, who pulled in his chin and raised his shoulders. Clearly, he didn't know she hadn't told anyone about leaving.

"Well, yes, Mom. We agreed from the beginning I'd go home once Lucas got discharged."

Beverly's bright expression deflated on the spot. "You've been such a big help around here," Beverly said. "And who's going to do my hair?"

That lightened the atmosphere and got a chuckle out of Lucas. "Don't look at me."

"Maybe you could teach me," Jocelyn said. She felt a bit foolish making the offer, especially when everyone, most especially Mrs. Grady, checked out her simple ponytail at once.

"How are you with a blow-dryer and hair spray?" Anne asked, an impish flint in her light brown eyes.

"It really is all about the cut," Beverly said. "And fortunately, I've got a good one."

"See?" Anne said. "All you'll need to do is wash, comb and fluff."

"Well, because Mrs. Grady's hair isn't long enough

for a ponytail, I guess I can learn to dry, fluff and spray."

"If you're going to be my hairdresser, you're going to have to learn to call me Beverly."

Jocelyn grinned. "Beverly." Would she ever feel comfortable saying Kieran and Beverly?

"What about Jack?" Kieran said. "Does he know you're leaving?"

"Dad, just drop it, would you?" Anne stood and picked up her plate, then her mother's, and headed to the sink.

With Jocelyn's help, Jack had convinced Anne to go out with him since she'd been home, and he'd been looking very happy the last couple of weeks. In Anne's defense, she did have a nursing job in Portland, Oregon to get back to—but Jocelyn was pretty sure Jack had bigger plans in mind.

No one looked more disappointed than Beverly. "It's been so great having you around, Anne. We just hate to see you go—that's all."

Jocelyn noticed the expression on Lucas's face, like he wasn't good enough to take Anne's place. She remembered that look from high school. Then he changed. Got tough. Used to brag about being a slacker.

She never believed him. Not for a second.

Wednesday morning, after Lucas helped Kieran get washed and dressed, he jumped into the shower. Midway through, a pounding on the door cut short the soothing hot ribbons of water streaming over his tense shoulders and back.

"Jack isn't answering my calls," Kieran shouted through the closed door. "We need to find another way to get to the doctor's appointment."

Lucas shut off the water, grabbed the bath towel and wrapped it around his waist in the thick-with-steam bathroom, then opened the door. "Why don't you give him another call in a minute or two? Maybe he's already on the road."

Today's appointment was important. It would clarify for Kieran when his leg cast might come off and, for a normally hyperactive guy, he was looking for a light at the end of this recovery. If he missed the appointment, it might be another month before he could reschedule.

His parents both owned hybrids, cars that had lots of attributes but weren't made for people with full leg casts. Especially six-foot-four people with full leg casts. Anne had mentioned that Jack had been providing his 1980s van for Kieran's transportation.

Lucas turned to wipe steam off the mirror.

"What the land's end is that?" Kieran said, as if he'd noticed a gaping wound on Lucas.

At first it didn't register, then it hit him. He'd turned his back on his father and exposed the tattoos. "Oh, these?" He played dumb and glanced over his shoulder as if he'd forgotten the raven on the backside of each shoulder blade existed.

"For cryin' out loud, are you serious? What got into

you? Next you're going to tell me you've taken up smoking again."

Lucas had actually put a lot of thought into his choice of tattoos. The ravens were Hugin and Munin, "thought" and "memory." According to Norse mythology, each morning Odin sent the birds out to the world to report back what they saw. Lucas preferred to think of his ravens as thought and reason—because he didn't put much stock in memories.

Sometimes, those ravens were the only things that kept him from having lousy judgment. Still, he saw that old and familiar look in his father's eyes. *Slacker. Only slackers get tats.*

Yeah? Well, you don't know everything, dear old Dad. But it wouldn't be worth the breath to explain how it felt to have men's lives balanced in your hands or how a wrong decision could cost a limb or eyesight or, worse yet, death. Dad wouldn't get it.

"For your information, I didn't start smoking again, and these are the only tattoos I have."

It's not like it's a dragon or demon or snake winding up my neck. They're ravens—just black birds. Okay, more like crows on steroids.

"The damn things nearly cover your back. Your mother will burst into tears when she sees them."

"Are you going to call Jack or what?"

On edge over the possibility of missing his appointment, Kieran momentarily put his judgment about tattoos aside, flipped open his cell and put his special electric wheelchair in reverse. At least for now, Lucas had gotten him off his back. Literally.

Ten minutes later, Kieran still hadn't reached Jack. Lucas ran next door.

He rapped on Jocelyn's door, and moments later she answered, looking surprised. "Hi, Lucas. What's up?"

She was dressed for teaching in a pin-striped pencil skirt, white blouse and black flats. Her hair was down and he liked how it gathered in fluffy bunches on her shoulders, but he wasn't here to gawk at her good looks. He'd come to get help.

"Sorry if I disturbed anything, but…" Lucas said, pulling back on track. "Does your dad still have that big old van?"

"Yeah. It's in the garage. Why?"

"Any chance we could borrow it?"

"No one has driven it in years. Probably doesn't even run."

Due to her confused expression, brows low, eyes narrowed, lips pursed—he especially liked that last part—he figured he owed her an explanation. "I've got to get Dad to his doctor's appointment in half an hour and Jack was supposed to pick us up and take us. He's a no-show."

"Oh," she said. "Yesterday afternoon Jack got a call at school to report for duty to fight the fire."

Anne had already explained how Jack was a teacher at the high school and a volunteer fireman for Whispering Oaks. Wait until Anne found out about Jack getting called in to fight the fire.

"Let me find the key," Jocelyn said. "Though the van battery's probably dead."

"I've got jumper cables."

She found the key hanging on one of multiple hooks in the laundry room and handed it to him. Their fingers touched and the pop of pleasure immediately grabbed his attention. "Let's see if it starts," she said, leading him into the garage. "If it does, it's yours."

"Thanks," Lucas said. "We really appreciate it."

Once in the driveway, Lucas couldn't help but notice how Jocelyn had to hike up her tight skirt in order to climb inside the van. Not wanting to tick her off, he averted his eyes after a quick appreciative glance.

He ran home to grab the jumper cables and to wheel his dad outside. On his way, he noticed a darkened sky with deep purple and red haze beneath and huge black clouds above a distant ridge. The wind had picked up instead of settling down, which didn't bode well for the firefighters, including Jack. Anne would be worried sick.

After he'd gotten a relieved Kieran inside the big old red van, with his leg cast stretched across the spacious back bench seat, Lucas loaded in the wheelchair. He closed the heavy door and turned, almost bumping into Jocelyn. Up close she smelled really good, like marshmallows and flowers.

He stretched the orange cables from car to van. "Pull your car up and leave the engine running," he said.

Lucas gave her a thumbs-up and Jocelyn started the car engine. "Now the van!" he called.

Lucas watched Jocelyn hike up her skirt again in order to slip behind the steering wheel. This time Lucas let himself enjoy the whole, long-legged show. When his eyes kept moving upward, he realized he'd been caught.

Jocelyn glanced at her lap before her lashes fluttered back up and she looked into his eyes. There went another mini jolt right through his chest—better than caffeine.

A tiny mischievous smile accompanied her glance as she turned the key and the old behemoth engine coughed and sputtered to life. Their eyes met and held a few moments, and he wondered if she felt what he was feeling. *Turned on.*

"Come on, you guys, or we'll never make it on time," said Mr. Personality from the backseat.

Lucas shot up in the dark, panting, drenched with sweat. There was fire. He smelled it. Where the hell was he? Clutching his chest, heart pounding in his throat, he searched frantically for a clue, but he had to wait for his eyes to adjust to the dark. It was too soft to be in a sleeping bag on the desert floor. Besides, he had a pillow, and he never had a pillow out there.

Right. He was home, at Whispering Oaks. It was two in the morning on Friday. There were wildfires in the distant hills. He was okay.

With adrenaline crawling along his arms and legs, he threw back the covers. He needed mindless tinker-

ing. Keeping busy. Distraction. Anything to keep from
thinking.

His pulse slowed a fraction as he headed for the
kitchen. He avoided the creak in the hall floor outside
of Anne's bedroom so as not to wake her.

After he got his drink, when he stepped outside, he
came to a halt. Something had changed. The wind had
stopped. He glanced across the backyard to a glowing
orange ridge in the distance. Maybe now the fire would
settle down, too.

Letting the last of his nervousness drizzle out, he
opened the garage door and got to work changing out
the headlights on the car.

Time slipped by and, as had been the early morning
routine since he'd been home, Anne eventually showed
up. Tonight she had an old high school yearbook in her
hand and a melancholy expression in her eyes. She'd
tried not to be obvious when she found out about Jack
fighting the fire today, but Lucas could tell by the way
she bit her nails and twisted her hair all evening that
inside she was freaking out. Something big was going
on between her and Jack.

He glanced at his sister, hair every which way, night-
gown hanging loose nearly to the floor, looking like
some kind of messy angel. She climbed into the Mustang, talking about anything that seemed to pop into
her head. It led back to high school and a love triangle
between Anne, her best friend at the time and Jack. He'd
tried his best to stay out of that drama back then but
still recalled the heartache his sister had lived through.

When she started what he called the remember game, he tried to keep up, knowing she might throw in a curveball pop quiz. So far, the first few questions she'd thrown at him had been slow and down the center.

"Remember the night before I left for college when I came and sat here and told you that I still loved Jackson Lightfoot but I could never have him?"

Was he supposed to remember those kinds of conversations? "Uh, kinda."

She went dramatic, tossed back her head and groaned. "Damn, Lucas, I break open my heart and spill my guts to you and you don't remember?"

"I didn't say I didn't remember. I just said it's a little vague. Why don't you run it by me again?"

And she did, boy did she, the whole sordid tale, which went on for at least fifteen minutes. He kept busy with the headlight, eyes nearly glazing over. Finally, things got around to the real reason she couldn't sleep.

"The thing is, I never quit loving him…"

So this was her bombshell? Hell, he could have told her that. Now all she had to do was be practical.

"Then why not move back here and be with him?"

For his effort of listening to and supporting his sister by offering a solution, he got the death glare.

"Ugh. It's not that easy."

"Sure it is," he said. "What do you have in Portland that you can't find here?"

She sighed and, ignoring him, thumbed through the yearbook.

Several minutes slipped by in silence. He was okay

with that. It allowed him to work on the headlight change in peace.

"Do you believe in people finding the love of their lives, Lucas?"

"Nope." He knee-jerked his answer as he used a wrench to tighten a bolt, then thought about Anne and Jack and what she'd just confessed. "But maybe in your case…"

Not answering, she closed her eyes and hugged that ancient yearbook to her chest. A moment later she got out of the car. "Thanks for listening, little brother."

Lucas loved his sister. He'd probably never said the actual words *I love you, Sis,* but right now he felt her pain and wanted her to know he cared. He gave her the first genuine smile he'd made since coming home, besides the one for Jocelyn, and it reached all the way inside, warmed him up and felt pretty damn good. He rubbed at a foreign, dull tugging in his chest.

"And by the way—" Anne said, closing the car door "—when you get ready to find the love of your life, may I suggest that you start by looking next door?"

He threw the greasy rag he'd wiped his hands on at her as she brushed past him on the way out of the garage. A ridiculous notion. Yet his eyes drifted across the dark yard to the house on the other side of the fence, and in his mind's eye a long pair of shapely legs came back into focus.

Chapter Three

Saturday morning, Lucas showed up for track practice like he told his father he would. It was already sunny at quarter to eight, no wind, mostly blue sky with left-over smoke in the distance along with a lingering sooty scent. He checked his watch. Where were the athletes? More importantly, where was Jocelyn?

He paced the length of the track, pieces of memories patching through his thoughts. *Just focus on the race. Give it your full effort.* He would swear his father spoke over his shoulder, though he knew Dad was home in the wheelchair where he'd left him—in the family room watching golf on TV. The poor guy was practically on house arrest.

How many times had he let dear old Dad down when

he raced? How many times could he have won and made Dad proud if he'd just three-stepped between hurdles instead of stuttering? But signing up for track hadn't been his idea. Anne had talked him into it, just so she could be around Jackson Lightfoot. Speaking of Anne, she'd never come home last night. Last he'd heard, she'd gone looking for Jack at the fire command center.

More thoughts rushed his mind as he walked the track. Back in high school, Lucas hadn't yet learned the fine art of total focus, except for when it came to cars. Being the coach's kid meant having to prove yourself, and it seemed that in his father's eyes, Lucas never really did. Second place was only a quick flash on Kieran Grady's track radar; third place didn't register at all. At least that's how it'd felt.

Lucas shook the bitter memories from his head.

What the hell was he doing here? Jogging on this track was like reliving his slacker days all over again. It felt idiotic. Old insecurities laced through him, quickly followed by anger. He wanted to punch something or kick over a hurdle and storm off, just like he used to.

Here he was, honorably discharged from the army, a medic, twenty-eight years old, no plans, no job, subbing for his dad for some stinking high school fund-raiser. He squinted into the sun. In some ways he still felt an L was tattooed on his forehead.

Ambushed by frustration, he burst into a sprint, slowed down a few paces, then sprinted again. Maybe he could run off the negativity.

"Lucas!" Jocelyn came trotting across the grass wearing running gear and holding her workout bag in one hand, long strides accentuating the tone and muscle of a female athlete. He could get used to looking at those legs, all right.

"Hey," he said when she got ten feet away, chiding himself for being so glad to see her.

"Sorry I'm late."

"Where're the kids?"

She checked her watch. "They should start straggling in any time now."

"That lack of discipline flies with my dad?"

"Nope," she said, plunking her overstuffed gym bag on the nearest bleacher seat. "They're taking advantage of me. They think I'm a softy because I don't blow my whistle and yell like he does."

"Dad would turn over in his wheelchair if he found out."

She laughed, way overdone for his lame comment. Her laugh sparked a déjà vu zing back to when he used to tease her. Good old Joss used to let him bug and nearly torture her, and she'd think it was funny. The sound of her laugh had grown huskier over time, but the sweet nature of it hadn't changed at all. A smile just sort of popped up on his face. She smiled back, and something about being here with her made his shoulders relax.

"Well, I guess I'll have to crack the old whip on my dad's behalf, then," he said.

She put her hands on her hips and raised her brows

above her sunglasses. "You do remember being exactly the same as these kids, don't you?"

"I've made it a point to erase my entire four years at Whispering Oaks."

"That's a pity because we had some good times. At least I thought so." She'd leaned over to stretch out her hamstrings, so he figured he should do something, too, besides ogle. He grabbed his foot, drawing it flush to the back of his thigh, and enjoyed the long pull on his right quadriceps.

"It wasn't that bad, was it?" she asked, head between the V of her legs. Did she have a clue about the power of that pose?

His answer stuck in his throat, which was a good thing because his tongue had momentarily quit working.

A gaggle of teens rushed across the lawn, a few stragglers running behind, as if they'd all arrived on a bus together. Lucas was sorry Jocelyn had quit stretching in order to greet the students. He glanced at his watch—eight-fifteen. Dad would hit the ceiling, and because he'd filled him in on Jocelyn's insecurity about losing her athletic scholarship and feeling as if she had little right to authority, Lucas decided to step in and give her some back up.

Channeling his father, and avoiding Jocelyn's questions, he clapped his hands hard enough to make an echo. "Let's put a move on it. Come on. Practice started fifteen minutes ago."

Fifteen minutes later, four more teens swaggered in to practice. "That was sick," the most muscular one said.

"So epic," the lankiest replied.

"You're late, guys," Jocelyn said. "Start your stretching."

Her comments didn't register on their too-cool-for-track-practice attitudes. Lucas walked up close to them, and having borrowed his dad's favorite device, blew the whistle.

"Drop your bags and take laps." Lucas glanced at his watch. "You're almost a half hour late, so you four will stay an extra half hour." If he were still in the military, he would have started the sentence with "ladies."

The boys stood dumbfounded, kind of like adolescent dinosaurs, waiting for the message to travel from their brains all the way to their legs.

"Let's go, let's go," Lucas said, clapping his hands again. Jock number one nodded to the others. Begrudgingly, they dropped their gym bags and halfheartedly jogged around the track, bickering under their breaths.

After the forty or so teens finished their warm-ups, they gathered at the bleachers and Jocelyn made formal introductions. Lucas scanned the group and easily identified the four major food groups in high school: cheerleading-squad material, battling-the-diet group, Jocks R Us, and, last but not least, "I still haven't figured out how to work my body" bunch. He had to hand it to his dad—every year he was faced with the same material, yet he'd always managed to pull the team together, find the star athletes, sometimes in the most unlikely kids, turn the rest of the students on to team spirit and good sportsmanship and in the process reel in his fair share of track medals. No easy feat.

When Jocelyn introduced Lucas as Coach Grady's son, he heard one quiet comment in the vicinity of the jocks. "Figures."

He suppressed the threatening smile. Dear Old Dad ran a tight ship.

As Jocelyn timed her distance runners, she couldn't prevent her gaze from drifting toward Lucas. One of the hurdlers had stumbled and twisted her ankle. Without being asked, Lucas had come prepared and had already elevated the runner's leg and put an ice pack on it. That look of earnest concern blew her away.

She checked her stopwatch. What lap was that? Oh, gosh, she'd gotten distracted and lost track.

She glanced at the stopwatch then back toward Lucas, who was now laughing with a tall, scraggly, redheaded kid. The warmth in her heart doubled when she saw him encourage the boy to give hurdling a try, and to her amazement, the kid wasn't half-bad.

Lucas glanced in her direction, and their gazes met and held. He nodded. She'd have to settle for the subtle lip twitch he offered instead of a smile, but that was enough to send a marching brigade of chills over her shoulders. She wasn't sure what it was, but Lucas Grady had It with a capital "I"—and she'd known that since she was six years old.

This was the Lucas she'd always seen. The big-hearted guy he'd fought to conceal. She'd never let him get away with putting himself down. Not on her watch.

Before Lucas knew it, the two-hour practice came to an end. He finished wrapping an elastic bandage around the little runner who'd twisted her ankle and sent her home with RICE instructions—rest, ice, compression and elevation. Somewhere along the line, he'd abandoned his everyday thoughts and had become completely engrossed in being outdoors, enjoying the sunshine and coaching track. It felt good.

But as he thought of heading home with no particular plans other than helping out his parents, a huge dreary cavity opened up deep inside. He'd tried meeting one of his high school buddies for a beer one night, but they couldn't relate to each other anymore. Lucas's world had expanded to include faraway deserts, death and mayhem and his buddy had finished college and spent most of his time at the bar complaining about not yet finding his dream job. Not once did the guy ask what it had been like to go to war, and Lucas sure as hell wouldn't bring up the topic. He went home feeling even more alienated—and then he had another crazy dream. Maybe tonight he'd have better luck sleeping.

"You were such a big help today, Lucas," Jocelyn said, jogging his way. "I can't thank you enough. I think you really got the runners to buckle down."

Little Miss Sunshine, acting like he was the greatest gift on earth. Didn't she get it? He was messed up. Always had been, but even more so now. He didn't belong here. He didn't belong anywhere, and he really didn't want to be forced to be around Jocelyn, the perennial cheerleader.

"No problem." His jaws locked, and the old and familiar tension in his shoulders returned. "I'll put the hurdles away, then I've got to get back home," he muttered, feeling as though the leftover ashes from the big fire hovered around him—like that character from Charlie Brown, Pig-Pen, but instead of a cloud of dirt and dust, his was gloom.

"You know, I'm barely holding it together," she said. "Your dad always works wonders."

He stopped, turned and gave her his full attention.

"I guess what I'm saying is, I can't wait for the big guy to get back, but in the meantime, I'm really glad you're around to help."

He wanted to ignore her, wanted to disappear. But he knew she was insecure about taking on the job, and from the unruly lot of athletes she'd inherited, she sure as hell could use some back up.

"Why wait for my dad? Why not work your own wonders?"

She pulled in her chin as if the idea were preposterous. After a moment or two of obvious consideration, switching weight from one hip to the other, opening her mouth once or twice as if to speak but nothing coming out, she shrugged. "I'll see what I can do."

"There you go." He winked, turned and, back on task, jogged toward the storage bin where the lanky kid with possibilities waited with the practice hurdles to help put them away.

"I'll see you Monday at four?" she called out.

"Yup," he said, over his shoulder.

"Ah, the magnificent smell of formaldehyde," Jocelyn said to herself, opening up her classroom lab at Whispering Oaks High on Sunday afternoon as the stale, toxic wave hit her nostrils. "Think I'll leave the door open."

The empty room stood forlorn, in need of filling up. Rows of student desks seemed eerily vacant. She'd come in to set up for the big anatomy test on Monday. She hadn't been at all sure she wanted to be the anatomy instructor a year ago when she'd transferred over from her substitute teaching job at Marshfield High. When she'd blown her free-ride athletic scholarship, she transferred to the state college and got her teaching degree in science. Then Whispering Oaks needed an anatomy teacher, so here she was teaching elementary science and college prep anatomy/physiology.

No longer a fill-in for a teacher on maternity leave, but a full-time science teacher, she was track coach, too.

She went about setting up for the test in quiet serenity, random thoughts popping in and out as she did. Yesterday, Lucas had been a natural at coaching. He was young, buff and gorgeous enough to keep the attention of all the girls, yet jock enough to challenge and command respect from the guys. He'd also accidentally discovered the natural talent of redheaded Brian Flaherty. Who knew the kid was a hurdler waiting to be outed?

Jocelyn shook her head. She'd spent far too much time thinking about Lucas since he'd gotten home a week ago, and it hadn't been that long since she'd broken off her engagement. What a disaster that had turned out to be.... She stuck a red-tipped pin into the gastrocnemius muscle of the lab specimen, near the Achilles tendon. The poor stiff cat bore the expression of the famous Edvard Munch painting, *The Scream.* They all did—all ten of them—in various stages of dissection. Sometimes she preferred biology labs to anatomy. Dissecting frogs wasn't nearly as grotesque as the cats.

Before Jocelyn realized it, two hours had passed as she painstakingly pinned numbered paper markers inside the formaldehyde-fixed innards of the cats for the midterm anatomy test. The smell had given her a headache, and she still had one cat left to label. Tomorrow morning she'd come in early and place the numbered note cards with the test questions by each pan.

She needed to get things set up for the non-honors basic anatomy class, too. Every year she'd have the students outline themselves on butcher paper, and as they studied each organ, they'd place it inside the body outline where it belonged. The life-size study aid could be rolled up and taken home, too.

Her eyes burned and got teary beneath the mask. If she wasn't wearing surgical gloves, she'd blow her nose. Being an anatomy teacher might be an unglamorous profession, but it was her job and she gave it her best effort. She'd learned her limits at the university when she couldn't give one hundred percent to her athletic scholarship and still manage to keep up with the academics. Although it was the hardest decision of her life, she knew that a sports career would be short-lived, whereas her education would last a lifetime. That had to come first.

How many other people at age twenty-seven could say they were content with their jobs and mean it?

But was she really happy, or was she just settling for content?

Why not work your own wonders?

Lucas's challenge jarred her. She'd been settling for stand-in status with track while subbing for Coach Grady, merely holding things down and waiting for him to get back. Was it because of her painful failure in college? She'd matured now, could focus more. Maybe it was time to *own* the position, put her name on it.

Work your own wonders.

Yeah, that's exactly what she'd do...that is, if it was okay with Mr. Grady. Uh, Kieran.

After a few more finishing touches, and meticulous hand washing, she was ready to leave for home. Her parents' house held a lot more appeal since Lucas had come back last week. If she were lucky, she'd get to see him again today.

Hmm, maybe Beverly needed her hair done...

An hour and a half later, after she'd washed and blow-dried Beverly's hair while hatching her plan, she knocked on Lucas's bedroom door with determination.

She needed his help. Honestly.

* * *

Minutes later, Lucas glanced down at Jocelyn sprawled out on top of a long sheet of butcher paper on the hardwood floor of the Howards' family room. She handed him a pencil.

"I need you to trace my body."

Three seconds ago he'd watched her on all fours with her backside up in the air, while she unrolled and smoothed out the thick brown paper. Now, her long legs lay beneath him in form-fitting jogging shorts. His gaze trailed upward, grateful she'd put on a T-shirt over the black sports bra, which was outlined through the thin white material. One slender arm reached out, extending a black wax pencil to him.

"Outline?"

She smiled up at him, oblivious to the battle she'd ignited between his head and body. Good old Jocelyn, the little girl next door versus the come-hither sex kitten stretched out on butcher paper reaching for him.

"I do this every semester," she said, sounding like usual but looking anything but. "I used to have Rick help me, but..."

He took the pencil. "Every semester." A crazy pinch of jealousy over Rick outlining her took him by surprise.

"Yeah. I have every student do the same thing in class. Then, as we learn about each system, we add organs to our 'bodies.'" She used air quotes. "By the end of the year, they have a great study aid for the final exam." She bent one knee and casually crossed the other over it, folding her arms across her chest. Maybe she did have a clue because he'd forgotten his manners and had stared at her chest for the past few seconds.

He cleared his throat, forcing his eyes upward to her face. "So where should I start?" His voice sounded foreign as she resumed the position and he dropped to his knees.

"You can start at my head." She beamed an encouraging smile. She couldn't possibly know how awkward this felt, not to mention the sexy visions flashing through his mind.

The room became deadly quiet except for the crinkling of butcher paper and his breathing. Their eyes caught for an instant. His fingertips tingled, and he quickly looked away. She finished repositioning herself into the dead man's pose with legs outstretched and arms at her sides.

Lucas kneeled over her and began to trace, focusing on the work and not the person. Her hair was fine, rich brown and lustrous, with emphasis on the lust. Geez, he'd been watching too many TV commercials since he'd gotten home. Lustrous? Her neck was long, like that of a ballet dancer. The only reason he knew about ballet dancers' necks was because Mom had talked him into watching *Black Swan* with them last week. Her shoulders were broader than most women's, but not manly-broad, definitely not. Hell, she was an athlete, so what did he expect?

Her arms only gave the impression of being thin. Fine muscles overlapped and cut a subtle, sturdy shape that made him want to touch them. *Show me what you got.* He was careful not to make contact with her skin, only allowing the thick-tipped pencil to do that.

Do not look at her face or into her eyes.

He concentrated on the task at hand.

"I want them to be together," she said. Her husky voice broke the stretching silence.

"What?" He looked at her face—*damn*—and into her eyes—*crap.*

"Anne and Jack. Have you noticed the chemistry between them?" She stared at the ceiling, and he was grateful she didn't see how closely he examined her mouth as each word rolled out.

He cleared his throat. "I haven't been around them much." Realizing he was hovering over her in a lover's position, he sat back on his haunches. "But I noticed how preoccupied Anne has been. She's been real touchy whenever anyone brings up Jack's name." He went back to outlining her torso, hip and bare-fleshed thigh, wishing for a longer pencil. Anything to avoid touching her skin. "She missed her plane yesterday, but Jack took her to the airport today."

"Great. Maybe they can trade weekends for a while until they…"

Three quarters of the way down her thigh, his thumb made contact. The surge of electricity shot up his fingers and into his arm. "Sorry." He quickly traced the safe region of her bony knee. Dimples? Her kneecap had dimples. Had he ever seen cute kneecaps before?

A safe distance from her eyes and steady gaze, he

traced down to her ankle and her bare feet. A soft pink pedicure made him smile. What would she do if he ran his fingers over her toes?

"You think they'll ever get together?"

His little fantasy dissolved. "No way of telling. Anne's pretty stubborn." The pencil began its journey up the inside of her leg. Satiny-smooth flesh waited to be traced. He swallowed hard. Three-quarters of the way up her inner thigh, the pencil made a sharp left turn, as if it had a mind of its own, making a saggy square-bottom effect. She didn't really expect him to go all the way, did she?

He began the descent back to her other knee and foot, taking a second look at the pretty pink nail polish, around and up the outside of her leg, as attractive as the other. She must have realized what she'd asked him to do was torture. Since when had little Jocelyn Howard become a tease?

"So, you're enjoying it?" He'd ventured back onto all fours, hovering over her again, catching himself and his breath as he looked below into her face. Her eyes registered surprise. "Teaching anatomy. Being a science teacher."

"Yeah," she said, as if mesmerized. "Turns out I love it."

"Great." He traced the last part of her head and sat back, hands on his thighs, to check out his handiwork, but more so to admire the person lying on top of it. "There you go." Damn, there went more quick and sexy strobe light poses and skin flashes through his mind.

He rose to his knees and crossed his arms to keep his hands from getting him in trouble.

Jocelyn rolled over and sat up to join him in looking at the silly, wavering outline of a saggy, square-bottomed figure. It resembled crime scene art—nothing remotely as fine as Jocelyn.

"Not exactly Van Gogh," he said.

"It'll do. Thanks so much," she said with a smile and a warm hand on his shoulder. It was the first time she'd touched him, not counting the quick and awkward hug at his house the other day, and the spark down his spine got his full attention.

"Yeah, well, it looks nothing like its subject, but there you go, and you're welcome." He handed the wax pencil back to her and scratched his forehead as he stood and stared at the butcher paper body rather than connect with her gaze.

She giggled. He glanced in her vicinity. She smiled a warm, pleased smile, light glistening off her lip gloss. The look and those lips felt like sabotage. "Maybe we should draw a happy face on it?" he said, a sorry attempt at humor.

"Nah, I have to leave room for the brain."

Speaking of brains, he wondered where the hell his had gone. A quick survey revealed it hovered somewhere below his belt. If he sprinted home, it wouldn't be fast enough.

Chapter Four

Lucas completed the Wednesday-afternoon pharmacy run for his father by driving past Whispering Oaks High. Track practice was in full swing, and he spotted Jocelyn in a bright blue warm-up jacket and shorts, running a group of athletes through baton handoffs in front of the bleachers. He pulled to the curb, parked and got out of the car.

Hands tucked in his back jeans pockets, he started across the grass. He wasn't supposed to help every practice. What was his excuse today? He could give her an update on the fund-raiser, tell her how his dad had lined up a batch of vendors willing to donate money for some advertising space. Heck, he had the list in the car, so he trotted back to retrieve it. With a solid reason to barge in mid track practice, Lucas stood taller and headed straight toward Jocelyn.

The air was warm and the sky sunny; only traces of last week's fire scented the air. He'd forgotten how consistent the temperature was here at home compared to the huge swings in the desert. He never wanted to carry fifty pounds of gear in a hundred and twenty degrees ever again. He used to complain about the nearly constant wind in Whispering Oaks until he had his face pitted with sand in sixty-mile-an-hour gusts over there. Funny how getting out in the world changed a person's perspective.

Halfway to Jocelyn, a scream came from the right. He spun into the sound. A squat, muscular kid jumped around in obvious pain. Jocelyn ran to the agonized student.

"He was practicing starting out of the blocks and he twisted his hand," a taller boy with mayonnaise-white skin said while lingering beside his friend. "His finger's sticking out all weird."

Jocelyn reached for the student's hand as Lucas got closer. Even from here he could tell that, by the way the finger aligned perpendicular to the palm, it'd been dislocated.

"Oh, Brandon, this looks bad," Jocelyn said just as she noticed Lucas. "Hi! Hey, Brandon has jammed his finger. Can you take a look, see if it's broken or anything?"

Switching into medic mode, Lucas took the teen's hand in his, then looked him square in the eyes. Brandon's contorted face said it all. He was panicking, in pain and really worried about what would come next.

With a steady gaze, Lucas waited for the kid to notice him. One eye peeked out from tightly squinted lids. "It hurts like a mother..." he said, voice cracking.

"It won't hurt for long," Lucas said, studying the finger, positive it wasn't broken. How many times had he reduced fingers in the field? He couldn't count. Hell, he'd fixed dislocated shoulders too. "But you need to let me put it back in place."

Terror flicked through the boy's gaze. "No way." He yanked his hand back, then immediately regretted it as the pain must have surged, causing the boy to hop around and whimper again.

"Don't swing your hand," Lucas said. "It'll make it worse. Just let me fix it."

A crowd circled the two of them. Peer pressure and the need to look cool probably influenced Brandon's decision to listen to reason. "I gotta sit down first," he said, looking more like the mayonnaise color of his friend's legs by the second.

"Everybody back off," Jocelyn said, pushing the air with her palms and making the circle wider so he could take the few steps to the bleachers and sit. Even from this distance, and under these circumstances, Lucas noticed the fresh scent of her body gel—marshmallows and flowers. *Focus.*

Lucas stayed calm, confident. He knew how to end the pain right now, but he needed to get the kid to agree to let him reduce the dislocated joint back into place.

"I'm a trained medic from the army, and I can fix this for you right now. Will you let me?"

Brandon locked eyes with Lucas and must have seen what he needed to see because he gave a slow nod.

The instant Lucas got the nod, and before the boy could nod a second time, he used one hand to stabilize the base of the finger, holding the fingertip with the other hand, and in one quick jerk pulled in opposite directions, quickly realigning the pinkie finger back in place with a single crack. Brandon squealed like a girl, but the deed was done. Success.

Lucas smiled at the stunned boy. "You okay now?"

As if waiting to see if the pain was really gone, Brandon stayed perfectly still for a second or two. "Yes," he whispered, probably regretting the noise he'd just made in front of the entire track team. Lucas could imagine how many times his buddies would remind him of it and imitate his shame over the next few days. Teenagers were ruthless.

He kept hold of Brandon's hand as he searched for Jocelyn. She was right at his side. "I'll need the first aid kit so I can tape his fingers together. Don't want this baby to slip back out."

"Sure." Off she trotted to the bleachers, a stream of flowery scent in her wake. She was back before Lucas had a chance to thoroughly check out her legs.

"Here you go," she said, handing him the thick white tape.

He smiled his thanks and went right to work taping Brandon's pinkie and ring finger together. "Ice it tonight. Twenty minutes on and twenty minutes off for as long as you can," he said, popping and activating a ready-made ice pack from the first aid kit and handing it to Brandon.

"Can I go home now, Coach?"

"Not until you thank Lucas," she said.

"Thanks." The kid stood to leave, squat muscular legs still wobbly.

"No problem, man."

"I think I need to lie down for a while first." Mayonnaise buddy escorted Brandon to the bleachers.

"Keep the ice on your hand for ten minutes," Lucas shouted, giving the student an excuse to stick around until he got some color back in his cheeks and a way to help the kid save face in front of his team.

As Brandon reclined on the hard bleachers, Lucas followed Jocelyn back out onto the track field, whistle around her neck, ready to blow. She did. Unprepared, he flinched. "Hey, everyone, show's over. Get back to your assigned practice station."

Once the small crowd dispersed, she sent Lucas an appreciative glance. "I can't thank you enough."

"No biggie. I can do that in my sleep," he said.

"See? You're a natural. You've got all this experience, and it seems a waste not to use it."

"I've used it enough," he said, trying not to think about all the ways he'd been called into action as a medic over the past several years.

They walked side by side toward the high jump. "Ever think about sports medicine?" she said.

He laughed. "I think you've mistaken me for my sisters. I'm the slacker Grady, remember?"

She shook her head, disappointed in his self-deprecating routine. "You could do it, Lucas. You can do anything you put your mind to."

The sun glared above, forcing him to squint. A strong scent of freshly cut grass made his nose itch, and he let a sneeze fly. "I just put my mind to not sneezing, but I did, anyway."

"Bless you. And you know that's not what I'm talking about."

The sneeze jolted his memory. "Before we get in a debate about what I will or won't do, I actually came here for a reason. Dad has lined up all the donors for refreshments, food and decorations." He handed her the list from his back pocket. "You're free to stop by the party store and pick out whatever you want, 'cause he set up an account for the high school." He fished in his other back pocket. "Oh, and here's the menu from Mindy's Diner. Look it over. Let Dad know what you decide. He already told me what he thinks you should get, but I suggested he let you pick since he's making you run the whole thing."

"Thanks for having my back," she said, her usual easygoing smile back in place.

"You're welcome. He needs that info by Friday." He turned to leave.

"You really should consider something in medicine, Lucas," she said, sounding far too much like a high school counselor than the woman next door.

He cocked his head. "Says who?"

"Says me." Sassy and sweet.

Little Ms. Perpetual Cheerleader never gave up.

The next evening, Lucas heard the doorbell but didn't race to answer. His mother was perfectly capable of getting it. Besides, he was in the family office on the computer, perusing the local community college's on-line courses. He slumped in the chair, the weight of having to play catch-up feeling like a cement block on his shoulders.

Did he really want to start from scratch at his age?

He heard Jocelyn's voice and quickly minimized the computer screen. The last thing he needed was for her to catch him following up on their previous conversation. He didn't want to give her false hope. Maybe he would or maybe he wouldn't follow through. The decision was far from being made.

When he heard mumblings of conversation, curiosity got the best of him and he wandered down the hall, deciding he needed a drink of water. His dad and Jocelyn were engaged in quiet conversation on the huge circular couch in the family room. Bart sat at alert in case food might be involved.

His mom sat nearby, engrossed with the topic, whatever it was. "That's a great idea," she said.

"I thought so, too." Kieran beamed his I-am-a-great-man-with-great-thoughts smile, the kind that made deep grooves in his cheeks.

Lucas's mouth twitched. He did everything he could

not to react, not to be nosy, as he headed for the kitchen for a drink.

"Hi, Lucas!"

"Hey, Jocelyn," he said, feeling like a teenager again, almost expecting his voice to crack.

"You and Jocelyn are going to have to do some shopping for plain-colored, multiple-sized T-shirts," Kieran said.

Says who?

"Your dad got the shirtmaker to donate one of his tie-dyeing machines for our event, but his shirt prices are too steep. We won't make any money if we go with him."

"It was my idea to do tie-dyed shirts." Kieran continued to beam.

Lucas filled a glass with refrigerated water, then leaned against the appliance door. "So you're thinking high school kids are going to rush to make these sixties-style shirts?"

"If not them, their parents will. Remember, it's a family event," Kieran said. "Besides, it's for a good cause."

"The retro look is always in," Jocelyn said. "I've seen a few kids at school wearing tie-dye and peace symbols."

Lucas shook his head, realizing how out of it he was on the teen front. He didn't have a clue what the trends in teen wear were, and he didn't really care.

"I'll buy one," Beverly said. "Make sure you get

some of those extra long T-shirts so I can wear it over leggings."

"Good idea!" Jocelyn wrote it down.

These marvelous minds didn't need his input, not that he had anything to put in, so he slipped out the kitchen door and headed to the garage for the solace of his Mustang.

"Hi."

Twenty minutes later, with Lucas engrossed in installing the alternator, Jocelyn's voice drew him out of deep concentration. "Oh, hey. Get all the planning done?"

She nodded, a willowy silhouette at the doorway. "A lot of it, but I'd like to run some things by you, if you don't mind." He liked what he saw: a ponytail high on her head, a snug yellow T-shirt, soft navy workout pants and flip-flops. She did casual well. But that wasn't all—she was good with his father, knew how to handle him. He liked that, too. And Lucas had always admired her ability to know what she wanted, and to go after it. Sometimes he was downright envious.

"That's your and Dad's thing." He didn't stop what he was doing. "I think you guys have it all covered."

"What I mean is…" She came into the garage, leaning on one side of the car while he leaned on the other, the raised hood between them. "This Saturday, Whispering Oaks is hosting its first track meet of the season, and I was wondering if you'd help out."

He used a rag infused with pungent motor oil to wipe off the part he held. "Don't you have assistant coaches?"

"If you count Mr. Nixon the math teacher and Ms. Finch from PE who always help out at the meets, but never make it to practice…"

"Then you don't need me."

"It's a big deal to host the meet." Her brows twisted and her forehead wrinkled. "I'll have a lot more responsibility, and, I'll be honest—I'm nervous."

He stopped what he was doing and gave her all of his attention. "From what I've seen, you've got it all under control."

She chewed on her thumbnail. "That's how it looked when I was in college, too. Everyone assumed I was doing great, until I failed a couple of classes and still only gave a mediocre performance at the track meets."

"Your scholarship?"

"I had a free ride to college and blew it, Lucas. I had to work to pay my rent, even with the scholarship, and track had to come first. I never had time to study." She shook her head, as if reliving bad memories. "I couldn't do it all."

"That's all in the past. Don't you think it's time to let it go?" Oh, yeah, look who was talking. If he were Jocelyn, he'd kick his own shins.

"I try, but it was a tough lesson."

"And this relates to Whispering Oaks in what way?"

She sighed and rubbed her eyes with her palms. "I'm afraid I've taken on more than I can handle again.

Teaching. Coaching. Now the fund-raiser. I'm scared, Lucas."

"What you need to do is learn to say no."

"I know, I know. But it isn't every day the head coach gets laid up with a broken arm and leg." She took a few steps closer. "Listen, I don't want to beg, but it sure would be great if you could…"

"I'll be there. What time?" Spoken like a man who hadn't listened to his own lecture. Besides, now that he had learned about her fear of failure, he realized maybe she could relate to how he felt whenever he thought about starting college at twenty-eight. He could use someone around who could understand some of the lousy feelings he'd been having these days.

Relief, appreciation and one more thing flashed in her eyes. He could tell she wanted to hug him, but she fought it. She'd even started toward him but stopped and hugged herself instead.

"You're the greatest. Thanks so much."

"Not a problem," he said as the third thing popped into his mind—adoration. As misplaced as it was, she'd always adored him, even when he screwed up, which was practically all the time back then.

How could a guy deserve respect from someone as intelligent and sweet as Jocelyn when he still didn't know what he wanted to be when he grew up?

"Just your being there will give me confidence," she said as she turned to leave.

He'd forgotten how to believe in himself, yet here she was cheering him on, making him feel like a superhero, an imposter superhero with fake superpowers and one who had absolutely nothing to offer her.

Whatever, Jocelyn. Whatever.

"Here, take this," Kieran said from the kitchen Saturday morning as Lucas headed for the door. He'd just helped his father bathe and get dressed for the day. He snatched the whistle by the string as it hurtled through the air and went straight for his face.

Dad looked oversized for the motorized wheelchair, with one casted leg extending out so far they'd had to remove the footrest, and the opposite arm bent and in a cast dangling over the side. For a man meant to spend hours in the sun coaching his runners, and who had the craggy lines and sun spots on his face to prove it, being confined to a wheelchair seemed like cruel and unusual punishment. With another two to three weeks to go in that cast, according to the last doctor appointment, no wonder he was in such a foul mood most days.

"Make sure those Marshfield coaches don't push Jocelyn around. You got that?"

"Got it." The only thing Lucas was remotely interested in today was getting through the meet, being as much help as he could for Jocelyn. The reward included catching another glimpse at her legs.

"Oh. Take this too." Lucas caught his father's Whispering Oaks track coach ball cap and stuck it on his head backward just to bug the old man. Under Kieran's death-eye glare, Lucas straightened the brim over his forehead and left.

Forty-five minutes later, because he'd dawdled at the car parts store to put off getting to the track meet, Lucas cut around the Whispering Oaks bleachers. He spotted Jocelyn in conversation with a handful of coaches from the other schools and felt a little silly with the ball cap on and whistle flopping against his chest. Talk about being a poseur. Soon the teachers fanned out, each heading in a different direction and looking purposeful. From what he could tell, she had things under control.

She noticed him, and he lifted his palm. She waved, then lined up the first batch of runners at the starting blocks. A man in a jacket and tie with a flat straw hat stood nearby, stopwatch in hand. The guy called out. "On your mark…"

"Hey, Coach Grady. How's it goin'?"

Lucas turned to see Brandon, fingers still taped together and looking anything but anxious this time around. "How's the hand?"

A gunshot cracked through the air.

Lucas dove for cover under the bleachers. Anxiety exploded in his chest as if he'd taken a hit. Visions of vehicles thrown in the air in balls of fire and flashes of body parts flying and soldiers dying, released the dam and every last drop of adrenaline he possessed rushed out. He squinted his eyes tightly and tried not to go there, but he got thrown back into the middle of hell anyway. He had to get hold of himself. He had to assess the situation and see how to be useful for his men. Another gunshot. He had to take stock of how many injured soldiers needed his help and triage them. He had to quit shaking.

A crowd gasped, and screams and shouts filled his ears. The flashback faded and little by little he repossessed the moment.

"Coach Grady, come quick!" Brandon's eyes were wide, his face ashen gray again.

Lucas's vision spun in dizzy waves as he looked up.

What the hell was he doing eating dirt under the bleachers? It was only a track meet. They fired blanks to start the races. Heat burned up his face. How could he explain what had happened? How could he face anyone?

"Ricardo broke his arm! The bone is sticking out and everything," Brandon continued, oblivious to the fact that Lucas was on the ground under the bleachers.

Having something to focus on other than bad memories, Lucas got to his knees, then stood and dusted off his jeans. He trotted toward the crowd, realizing everyone was focused on one athlete, not him.

He locked eyes with Jocelyn, who looked startled. Of course she'd look concerned: the track meet had only just started and a runner was down. She probably didn't have a clue that he'd just time traveled eight thousand miles to Afghanistan.

Lucas worked his way into the crowd toward Ricardo. Whoa! The kid had a ragged-edged bone protruding through a tear in his skin, otherwise known as a compound fracture of the right arm. It was an ugly sight and probably hurt like hell.

"Has anyone called an ambulance?" Lucas asked,

dusting off his hands, quelling his internal trembles and accepting the first aid kit from another coach.

"They're on their way."

As Lucas opened the kit and used the hand sanitizer, he glanced around and realized this kid had only made it over the first hurdle before face-planting on the rough red Tartan track. Tough luck. Tough next six weeks, too, after surgery, which would include pins and plates to put the bones back in place. Just like his dad had gone through a month ago.

Knowing the EMT was on the way, Lucas cleaned the wound, gently wrapped it in gauze and splinted the arm with the small padded boards provided in the first aid kit to protect the break and save Ricardo from additional pain.

That evening, Lucas couldn't shake the blood-and-guts images popping into his head. He'd avoided being around his parents, knowing they'd catch on that something was bothering him and ask a bunch of questions. He'd jerked and flinched each and every time the starting gun fired at the track meet, even when he'd warned himself. A montage of bloody bones and flesh injuries looped through his mind, buddies covered in blood, dirt and soot, the kid's radius protruding through his skin. Gunfire.

He could take one of the pills the army doc had prescribed, but it would make him feel like a zombie, then put him to sleep, and tomorrow he'd have to face the same facts.

Rubbing his chest, he put on his running shoes and jogged toward the front door.

"Where're you going?" his mother called out from the kitchen.

"For a run."

He quickly stretched his thighs and hamstrings using the huge pine tree in his front yard, then set off at a slow jog, waiting for his muscles to warm up so he could sprint away the tightening coils of anxiety in his chest. If necessary, he'd run until it seared every muscle in his body. He'd run until he was so damn tired, he'd have to use all his energy and every bit of his concentration to limp home.

Eyes straight ahead, shoes thumping on the cement, emptying his mind, he focused only on what was ahead, putting one foot in front of the other.

"Wait up!"

He glanced over his shoulder, seeing Jocelyn sprinting to catch him. He wanted to be alone but couldn't very well run away from her. Grinding his teeth he slowed down and let her catch up.

"Mind if I tag along?"

Yes. He did mind, but what could he do? "Are you kidding—you'll probably outrun me."

They ran on in companionable silence for the next block, and Lucas hoped it would stay like that. No way was he going to start a conversation that he knew would lead to having to explain why he dove for cover. Unless she hadn't seen him.

Wishful thinking.

"I can't get Ricardo's broken arm out of my head," she said, not even out of breath.

"Yeah, it was a nasty break."

"I checked with the hospital and he's already had surgery. Everything should be fine."

"Good."

The long street was lined with ash trees that formed a pale green canopy overhead. A grand gnarled oak sat like a sentry at the corner.

A few minutes later they ran past the neighborhood grammar school they'd attended together, the one where Lucas's mother still taught. Man, nothing had changed except the color. The flat, fifties-style cubes used to be gray, and now they were beige. And the sign out front had a computerized running message in neon red instead of the old white-lettered announcements hand-placed by the vice principal.

"Let's go up here." Jocelyn pointed up a street dotted with pines that ended at the base of the nearby hills. She matched him stride for stride and never seemed out of breath. Impressive.

With each block they covered, the knot in his chest slipped looser and looser. He liked listening to Jocelyn breathe and catching whiffs of her shampoo or whatever it was that reminded him of Rice Krispies Treats. She'd challenged him up the hill and he wasn't about to concede defeat, especially after humiliating himself earlier today. A guy's manhood could only take so much embarrassment for one day.

"You want to talk about it?" she asked, edging ahead of him.

"Nope." He knew exactly what she meant, and he wasn't about to give her kudos for slyly introducing the subject.

She slowed down, let the topic lie for a few more strides. "I was focused on the race starting, but I was looking for you. You scared me. The look on your face. It was like you were petrified or something."

"I had a flashback."

"A flashback?"

"Comes with the territory. The starting gun set off my PTSD."

She stopped dead. "You have PTSD?"

"A lot of us do." He sped up, and she quickly caught him.

"So what do you do about it?"

"Get through it. Let it run its course. Hope it will get better over time."

She tapped his arm. "I had no idea, Lucas. You've seemed just like your old self until today."

His jaw gripped again. He hadn't been his old self since he left home. Wasn't that the point when you left home—to change?

They ran on, onto the dirt path cut along the hills. Wheat-colored grass and mustard plants with tiny yellow flowers covered the expanse. When he was a kid, he used to ride his bike as fast as the wind up here, trying to fly over the makeshift ramps he and Anne set up just to see how being airborne felt. Tonight, his legs felt like cement, but he wasn't about to let Jocelyn outrun him.

At the halfway point, his chest was burning but in a good way. With the evening breeze smoothing the tension in his face, he glanced at Jocelyn. She'd kept her mouth shut. Something about the way she didn't push him, and her undemanding wide-open eyes, helped loosen his jaw.

"Sometimes I have terrible dreams. I see guys with their limbs blown off or burned and in agony. Today the gunshot set me off, but sometimes I just fly off the handle for no reason. I used to feel so helpless when all I could do was try to stop the bleeding or dope up one of the soldiers, just to stop their pain until they could be transported. Depending where we were, sometimes it took forever to get them transferred to the MASH units." He glanced at her as those pretty brown eyes stared straight ahead, as if she knew if she made a peep he would shut up, and she didn't want him to. Well, she'd asked for it, and he would lay it all out there. Maybe then she'd get the point and leave him alone.

"Sometimes I want to beat my fists against the wall and yell because I can't take it anymore." He punched the air like a boxer prepping for a match. Was she scared yet?

She kept running by his side, gently watching him, leaving the conversation completely up to him.

"I've been thinking about reenlisting so I can go back where my hair-trigger reflexes make sense. I don't fit here in sleepy little Whispering Oaks anymore."

He noted a twist of her eyebrow and her mouth shut tighter, yet she still didn't utter a sound.

They ran back down their street, four feet beating the cement in syncopated rhythm. The sound soothed him. He glanced at her and saw the look she'd tried so nobly to hide, the look he didn't want to be responsible for. "All I do is worry people here."

They ran the rest of the way home in silence. He had to admit he felt like he'd hurled a brick load off his chest by opening up to someone who wasn't a shrink. He knew his parents wouldn't understand, and he didn't expect Anne to, either, but Jocelyn was different. He was broken, and he had finally admitted it to her out loud.

They came to a stop in front of his house, both sucking in air and sweating. It felt good. Cleansing. He needed the outlet and, not surprisingly, he liked her company. She'd helped him purge his thoughts. Maybe saying "I have PTSD" aloud would help make the condition go away.

If only it were that easy.

He leaned against the pine tree, a rueful smile twisting his lips. "You sure you want me to help with that fund-raiser? A balloon may pop and I might freak out on you or something." He tried to use humor, but it fell flat.

From nowhere her cool hands caressed his cheeks. Jocelyn went up on her toes to buss his lips, catching him by surprise.

"Yes," she said, gazing into his face. "I still want you to help me with the fund-raiser." There was a playful glint in her coffee bean-colored eyes. "I also hope you'll reconsider about reenlisting. Besides, your parents need your help." With her hands still framing his face, her lashes fluttered downward then back up.

Their gazes met and held in an I-refuse-to-be-the-first-to-look-away contest. He could hear her breathe, and there was that sweet flower bloom and vanilla shampoo scent again.

Chapter Five

Standing in Lucas's front yard beneath the tall pine, Jocelyn wasn't about to let him know how much she needed him. The night air sent a chill over her sweat-moistened shoulders. She hoped he didn't think their quick-as-a-firefly kiss was the reason for the goose bumps. Though it definitely was. She'd given the kiss because he needed to know she cared about him, and honestly, she'd wanted to kiss him since she was six years old. She could hardly call it a kiss—more like a preview.

A kiss with potential.

His coming home had brought back all the good memories she'd let slip from her mind when the re-lationship with her ex-fiancé had changed. That guys and girls could have fun together. That it was possible to care about someone for years and years, even when they were gone and never tried to get in touch. That there was such a thing as true friendship.

Rick had scarred her toward men. He'd changed in front of her eyes. Given what Lucas had just told her, wouldn't his circumstances make him a changed man, too?

She really should remove her hands from Lucas's beard-stubbled cheeks and quit staring into his darkening hazel eyes, but…

Lucas made a quick move for her mouth, covering her lips with his before she knew what he had on his mind. A kiss could really mess up their rediscovered friendship, but man-oh-man, it felt great. His mouth was warm and moist, soft and inviting. And dreamy.

Just as quickly as he'd moved in, he ended the kiss, right when she'd quit resisting and decided she wanted more.

He took a step back, distancing himself. She saw caution in his eyes, as if he were sorry for making a huge mistake. Was smashing lips in the middle of the sidewalk the right thing to do? She thought so, but he'd called the shots on this one.

Lucas had just opened up about his struggles—he'd valued her enough to show his emotional warts. She'd seen the panic in his eyes today as he dove for cover at the track meet. It had taken him four miles and lots of sweat to break down and tell her about his PTSD diagnosis.

He'd opened up to her, then followed it up with a kiss. The least she could do was share something with him. Something from her heart because sex was out of the question so soon after her breakup. Plus, she and Lucas were friends, first and foremost, lifetime friends. She wouldn't dare disrupt the ecology of their friendship with something as tempting as sex…with the sexiest guy she knew…who happened to be her next-door neighbor.

Feeling flushed, she glanced into his hooded eyes. Damn, he really was appealing, even now with caution written all over his expression. She wanted to touch his lips with her fingertips to see if they still felt warm, but she cleared her throat instead. Fighting to focus, she decided to open up to him. "You know I was engaged for six months, right?"

He gave a slow nod.

She glanced at her beat-up cross trainers then back at him. "My ex, Rick, was a football coach at Marshfield High, the first school where I taught. He liked that I was athletic, and I enjoyed going to all of his games. We started dating, then got serious and he asked me to marry him."

She looked at her shoes again, waiting for the right words to come, not wanting him to think she'd been a pushover. Lucas had gone back to leaning against the pine tree and drinking the water she'd offered from her runner's waist pack.

"It was pretty innocent at first. He challenged his team to buff up, and they all worked out together at the local gym several times a week. He got great results, but that wasn't enough for him, and he started taking steroids." She paused, remembering. "Within half a year he'd changed drastically—he was humongous. I really didn't care for the look, but he was totally into it, so I kept my thoughts to myself. Didn't want to hurt his feelings."

Bad memories of his twisted face pushing into hers, yelling at her like a drill sergeant, trying to scare her— and doing a damn good job of it—made her draw a shaky breath. She cleared her throat. "He started to bully me."

Lucas straightened and cocked his head.

"He never hit me or anything, but he pushed me down once. And he scared me. I didn't know him anymore, and I didn't like what he'd changed into."

She saw alarm in Lucas's on-alert eyes.

"It only took the one push. I broke it off the next day. Got out of that apartment and moved back home."

Damn it, she really didn't want her eyes to well up in front of Lucas, but they burned and went bleary anyway. He cupped her arm. She leaned into his hand. "I made a bad choice turning my head to his steroid use and what he'd become, and I got zapped with the consequences."

She caught his gaze, wise with a history of mistakes, and relaxed into the hazel softness. Of all the people she knew these days, he was the one who could understand.

"Seems to me you made the right choice that day."

She nodded solemnly and scratched the prickles on her neck. "Only when push came to shove. Literally." She stared at his broad shoulder because it took too much confidence to look him in the eyes, confidence she was sorely lacking. "I'm scared to death about taking on the head coach position because I've failed at so many things I've tried to do before."

"Everybody screws up sometime." He shrugged and an ironic smile twitched at the corners of his lips. "Hell, look at me. I'm the king of screwing up."

She laughed and kicked a small rock, grateful he'd understood.

He moved infinitesimally closer. "You did great today," he said, his voice soft and solid. "You've got what it takes to make it happen. You're trained. Organized. Easy to work with. You've just got to believe in yourself."

She swallowed and blinked away the moisture. "Ditto, dude."

He lifted his brows, gave a *touché* smile and squeezed her arm the teeniest bit tighter.

She chanced a glance, found his dizzying eyes and locked on. "So here's what I'd like to throw out there," she said, her voice a bit breathy. "I'd like to be there for you if you ever need to talk, but that doesn't come without strings." She stared deeper into his eyes, now shadowed by moonlight and dim stars. "Would you be willing to be my sounding block, too? I mean if I start to panic and feel like I'm sinking or something with all of this stuff going on? Could you be that for me?"

"Your wingman?"

"My backup."

His hand dropped from her arm. He pushed off from the pine tree and stretched his neck, as if tossing a sudden weight.

It may have been a major mistake, but damn, it had felt good kissing Jocelyn. He'd done it on reflex because she'd kissed him first. He'd only sampled a taste before Mr. Cota came by walking his dog. No way could he start a relationship these days, and with Jocelyn, the kiss would definitely get blown out of proportion. It was best to nip things in the bud.

How hard was it to listen when a person needed to talk? He'd been doing it for the past hour or so, just the two of them under the night sky, confessing their biggest weaknesses. Even though he'd tried to shut down the conversation with a kiss, they really *had* opened up to each other. Though it went against his solitary nature, her soft brown eyes compelled him to try to be there when she needed him. At least for as long as he stuck around Whispering Oaks.

"I'll try, Jocelyn." He'd never been good at rah-rah dancing for his sisters, either. "That's the best I can offer right now."

Her gaze flicked over his face. "Then that's good enough for me." Her usual sassy bravado returned as she patted his T-shirt, damp from sweat. "Thanks for the run…and the kiss."

That got his attention. "Hey, you started it."

She shook her head, a puff of air replacing an outright laugh. "After the headache of today's track meet, I guess I needed to let off some steam."

"I know a boatload of better ways to let off steam." *But not with little Jocelyn Howard, the girl next door, idiot.*

She laughed outright and turned to walk home. "I'm sure you do," she said without looking back. "Maybe sometime you can show me, but we both reek right now."

That got a smile out of him. He stayed standing by the pine tree, watching her saunter back to her house and thinking about what had just happened, starting with that innocent comfort kiss.

After she went inside he dropped back his head, rolled his shoulders and thought how much lighter he felt.

He saw the curtain flutter at the corner of his living room window. Mom had most likely seen the whole kissing business and hadn't wanted to break up anything. Aw, cripes, now he'd never hear the end of it.

He glanced at his watch. Damn! It was way past his father's bedtime and he'd probably be champing at the bit to go to sleep.

With a sigh, Lucas pushed off the tree and headed for the front door, one lingering thought in his brain. *Not bad, for a first kiss.*

Lucas had spent Friday afternoon helping erect booths while Jocelyn directed the pep squad on the decorations at Whispering Oaks High School. They'd both been so busy they'd hardly had a chance to talk to one another, and it was probably best. All that opening up the other night had been exhausting. He'd spent the past decade surrounded by men. Communication wasn't high on the list of their skills, at least for most of them.

From what Lucas had observed, Jocelyn had everything under control, even when outside vendors started showing up and squabbling over prime property for the best foot-traffic flow.

He'd forced Jocelyn to go home with him around 4 p.m. to clean up and get ready for the evening. She'd thanked him for the millionth time for all of his help when they parted paths at her driveway. He'd waved her off, acting blasé, yet admitting a certain sense of pride in his part of the fund-raiser. When he'd gotten out of the shower and wandered to the kitchen for some iced tea a half hour later, he glanced next door to her driveway and noticed her car was already gone. Typical. She gave a hundred-and-twenty percent.

An hour later, Mom and Dad were dressed and ready to go. In honor of the sixties theme, Lucas opted for the timeless look of threadbare jeans and a ripped T-shirt. Despite others claiming it thirty years later, the sixties had pioneered the grunge look and he'd wear it with pride. His mother had a whole other look going on, one he tried not to snicker over. Something more in tune with the cast of *Hair*. Or maybe a band of gypsies? Somewhere, she'd dug up dangling peacock-feather earrings, probably from one of her fourth-grade craft projects, and a slinky, silk, knock-your-eyes-out purple blouse over her heavily patched vintage jeans. Even her brightly colored cast matched.

His dad wore a loud print neon orange and brown dashiki shirt, having to settle for sweatpants with one leg cut off to accommodate the hip-to-ankle cast, and a bright red neckerchief tied around his forehead. The man looked happy and ridiculous. Lucas wondered if this was how some of his older aunts and uncles had actually dressed during that era because his parents were mere toddlers when the Beatles had first invaded the United States.

Lucas had arranged to borrow the Howards' beat-up old van to transport his parents to the Friday-night fundraiser. Because it took so dang long to get his dad out of the van and set him up in his electric wheelchair, the event was well under way when they got there. Though Dad was making good progress walking with crutches on their daily physical therapy sessions, it was much easier to use the wheelchair for public outings.

Grace Slick reverberated off the stereo speakers singing about a rabbit as they entered the high school multi-purpose-recreation room. Incense burned at one booth, with a healthy line of students waiting to purchase some for themselves. Peace signs got flashed way too often amid noisy conversations. The tie-dye booth seemed to be a huge success judging by the long line, second only to the make-your-own-peace-beads stand. In the opposite corner, the timeless snack food of hamburgers, fries, soda and pizza also proved to be a hit at the never-out-of-style diner booth.

Dad had ceaselessly bragged all week how, according to Jocelyn, the decorating committee of students had planned the whole setup and done a marvelous job. Lucas knew her input and guidance had had a lot to do with it. Dad may have lined everything up, but Jocelyn organized the event down to the love-in atmosphere and too-cool-for-school ambiance.

In a nutshell, she'd nailed the sixties.

Someone had set up a "Guitar Master" booth exclusively playing Jimi Hendrix songs. Another booth offered Beatles karaoke sing-offs. The competing sounds could turn a person's stomach—or set off a PTSD moment—but Lucas let the happy students' faces keep him focused on why he was here.

Candle making, psychedelic black light paint spinning and face painting rounded out the event with something for virtually everyone.

With the help of some of his father's devoted students, who insisted on signing the coach's cast, Lucas left his mother to push his father around the multipurpose center and wandered around, taking everything in.

Lucas chuckled when he saw it and couldn't resist a go at a larger-than-life-size Jim Morrison cutout. He bought ten tickets and successfully tossed a beanbag through a hole in Jim's crotch while "Light My Fire" played in the background. The lanky kid from track, Brian, challenged him to a match. Each time either one of them made the shot through the crotch hole, Jim growled the infamous "Fire!" In the spirit of the night, Lucas let Brian win.

Across the room he spied Jocelyn, who'd gone for a flower-child look by wearing a flowing and colorful-patterned skirt and a bright orange tank top covered in layers of peace beads. Her hair hung loose and free beneath a wreath of baby's breath. She'd already had a flower painted on her cheek and a rainbow on her deltoid, and the effect took him by surprise. Wow. He dug it, from her huge hoop earrings right on down to the flower-power flip-flops. Going barefoot was prohibited at school.

She saw him and waved but immediately got pulled in another direction by a group of students. He killed some time at the paintball booth, creating gun-powered art on a huge canvas beside Brandon, the kid with the dislocated pinkie. Because he was the one pulling the trigger, the sound didn't bother him. Pop, pop, pop. Not bad for a guy who'd flunked out of art class.

Everyone seemed to be having a blast, and after Lucas scarfed down a burger, Jocelyn approached.

Wilson Pickett was waiting 'til the midnight hour, and Jocelyn grabbed Lucas's hand. "Dance with me?"

"I don't dance." He'd never been much good at it, and what he had known had endured a slow death from neglect.

She pointed to the dance floor with kids flailing themselves all over the place in no particular rhythm. Then he saw his mother gyrating some sort of sixties East Indian-influenced psychedelic movements in front of his dad's wheelchair, and his father doing the same kind of hand movements, and Lucas got shamed into accepting her invitation.

Feeling like a stiff oaf as the music changed and Janis Joplin screamed and squealed her way through a song, he let Jocelyn take the lead. She deserved to cut loose after all the stress she'd been under. This was her night, her success. Lucas went for understated and cool with his movements, which proved to be almost standing still with a few wrist flicks. Jocelyn looked far, far better as she danced, hot little flower child that she was. When a Van Morrison song came on he admitted that he could get used to watching his brown-eyed girl. *La la la...la ti dah.*

The silliness of the event eventually wore off on him, and he didn't even protest when Jocelyn talked him into getting a third eye painted on his forehead. Next, they took a picture together behind cutouts of super-sized hippie characters. He won her a bouquet of potted pansies at the strobe-light ring-toss challenge, and moving from booth to booth they poked fun at all the crazy stuff the sixties had ushered in. They laughed. A lot. He couldn't remember the last time he'd let go and enjoyed himself so much.

Now that he was hyped up on soda and a good mood, when she dragged him out on the dance floor again, this time for some Motown sounds, he finally cut loose and really danced, not caring what anyone thought about his strictly white-guy moves. Jocelyn kept up with him and his arm flapping as a sad excuse for dancing, move for move. Did they do hip bumps in the sixties? He didn't care. All he knew was that it was fun to bang against her hips. It brought to mind another kind of hip banging, and, well, he jumped around the dance floor in order to get past that image.

Amid the chaos, the diminutive principal, Cynthia Saroyan, older but even shorter than when he'd been a student here—if that were possible—took to the stage. Droning on in four-inch spike heels and an anachronistic business suit. Her announcements and thanks went on and on and on, nearly sucking the joy out of the room. Finally, she reminded everyone that the fund-raiser helped support the sports programs and then lifted a piece of paper. "Tonight we've already raised $15,000!"

Before he could fully process the total, Jocelyn jumped into his arms. Her body felt light, sturdy and wonderful, and it fit him well. He held her in place by hoisting her hips while a whole other scenario played out in his mind.

With her arms around his neck, her scream practically took out his hearing. When she pulled back long enough to grin at him—a beautiful grin that made him focus on her excellent mouth—he couldn't help himself and moved in for a victory kiss. Their mouths smashed together with enough momentum to knock teeth, but her sweetly padded lips softened the blow. Her arms tightened around his neck and he circled one arm around her waist, pushing her belly closer to his—then followed through on a wild and crazy lip lock that rolled through his center all the way down to his toes.

She kissed like she ran, intensely and purposefully, and he kissed her back to match her vigor. She angled her head and started a whole new warm and melting approach. His lips parted. She touched the tip of his tongue with hers, and he was instantly ready to take things to the next level.

Completely lost in their kiss, with every centimeter of his body participating and his nerve endings lighting up with neon bingo signs, the loud cheers and hoots and hollers broke his concentration. The invasive sounds pulled him out of the moment and placed his feet firmly back on the floor of the multipurpose room. He cracked open one eye and saw a circle of students closing in, and he immediately terminated the kiss, easing Jocelyn down so her feet could touch the floor. What the hell had he been thinking? Life was confusing enough now without throwing in a necking session with the girl next door...in front of a good portion of the student body.

Hell, he knew exactly what he'd been thinking as they kissed, and those thoughts were X-rated and nowhere near appropriate for a high school gym.

Jocelyn looked disoriented at first, but she quickly recovered, though she first passed him a sexy "wow" glance that seemed to promise to pick up where they left off later. He was definitely down for that. She clapped along with everyone else, so he joined in. Like several of the students, Jocelyn shot her fist in the air and yelled. "Woo hoo!"

Lucas faded into the crowd while she dealt with all of the congratulations and back slapping, giving himself a chance to process what in the hell had just happened. He'd felt that kiss like a hot rolling wave all through his body and he was damn sure Jocelyn had been as turned on as he was. If the students hadn't dragged her away with their cheering and excitement, he might have suggested they sneak off to a quiet place, and who knew what might have happened then?

In typical sixties vernacular, their kiss had blown his mind, and he'd never ever be able to look at Jocelyn as the sweet little girl next door again.

Chapter Six

"I'm sick of practicing with these crutches." Saturday morning, Kieran Grady looked glum and showed all the signs of restlessness—lack of concentration, irritability, absolutely no interest in trying—during his daily physical therapy workout.

Lucas faced him in the family room, hands on his hips. "You heard what the doctor said. You're stuck with the leg cast for another two weeks at least, so you may as well figure out how to use these special crutches." He held a regular crutch in one hand and the specially made crutch with an armrest extending from the top for his casted arm in the other. "Look, I know it's tough having your arm in a cast, too, but it's not impossible to do this."

"Easy for you to say." His father didn't look convinced, not by a long shot, but there was a tiny spark of interest in his eyes. Maybe Lucas was making some headway—he just had to find the right angle to lure in his father.

"Two more weeks, Dad, and that cast will come off."

"And then what—walk with a limp the rest of my life?"

Lucas understood why his dad was in a foul mood. The loss of his Harley, his broken bones and his inability to coach the track team had been tough on him, and the road to recovery seemed long.

Lucas was glad to help out, especially because he still didn't have a clue what he wanted to do next with his life. Any excuse to continue putting off "finding himself" worked for him.

"If you're committed to physical therapy, you'll stand a good chance of getting back to your old self."

"My old self is old, too! I'm fifty-five. Track and field requires a fit coach, not a slug. Truth is, I'll never be like I used to be."

"Never say never. Isn't that what you used to tell me?"

For all his effort, Lucas received an exasperated harrumph from his dad.

His younger sister, Lark, was finishing up her first year in medical school and had called home just this morning saying she was coming for a visit in a few weeks. Lark had become the light of her dad's eyes soon after she was born, especially after he realized Lucas had no intention of fulfilling all those educational plans he'd made for him. She'd been Kieran's little blond-haired, blue-eyed angel all her life. Compared to his sisters, Lucas was definitely the odd man out.

No way would Dad want Lark to see him like this—weak and cranky and unable to walk by himself. Yet Dad wasn't trying at all today, and it was up to Lucas to motivate him. Hmm, something seemed reversed in this equation. Maybe this was how frustrated his dad had felt back when Lucas was in high school and slacking off at just about everything…except for auto shop.

"Look, I know it was hard to see Mom get her cast off yesterday, but her break wasn't nearly as bad as yours. You've got rods and plates in there." He pointed to his father's left leg. "The ortho doc promises you'll lose this in another couple of weeks, just in time for when Lark comes home." He glimpsed a spark of inspiration in his father's eyes just before it fizzled. "Listen, I've got a plan."

Kieran cast a skeptical blue gaze. Lucas had seen that same blue-eyed look a gazillion times from Lark whenever he'd tried to talk her into something she knew wasn't a good idea. Like the time he'd tried to convince her to do a cannonball into the duck pond on the golf course two blocks over. Lucas had had a lot of sketchy plans growing up.

"How about a change in scenery?" he said. "Let's move this session outdoors."

By the tilt of Kieran's head, Lucas knew his idea had some merit.

"I'm sick of the house and the backyard. How about you?"

"To death," Kieran said with a concurring nod.

"Then let's take this show on the road. We'll go out front and you can amaze your neighbors with your prowess."

"What if I fall on my keister?"

"I'll pick you up. Better yet, I won't let you get that far."

After a moment's hesitation and a flinty steel-blue stare, Kieran said, "It wouldn't hurt to get some neighborhood support. They probably all think I died or something. Let's go show 'em what I'm made of."

Ten minutes later, Lucas had to use every patient cell in his body to counter the insecurity radiating off his father. "You've got it, Dad. Concentrate. First move the crutches, then swing your good leg."

"It's so damn awkward."

"I know the cast messes this up a bit, but don't be afraid to put weight on that armrest. It's supposed to distribute the weight evenly. And don't put weight on your armpit on the other side. Use your good hand to hold you up."

"Since when did you become such an expert?"

"I'm a medic, remember?" He'd been a medic for eight years, but to his father the only ones serious about the medical profession were Anne and Lark.

"I've been thinking," Kieran said.

Lucas kept quiet, not wanting to interrupt whatever his father planned to say.

"Maybe I should think about throwing in the rag with coaching track. It's such a big responsibility. I'm tired of it. Maybe it's time to let someone else take over and I can just be one of the assistant coaches. Not having to run the show. You know?"

"That's your call, Dad. You know what's best, but maybe think about it some more."

"Think? That's all I've been doing, lately."

From the corner of his gaze, Lucas noticed the movement of a certain lithe and sexy body in the yard next door, and his frustration and concentration dissolved. Jocelyn appeared out front preparing for her daily jog, lunging and stretching first one leg and then the other. Next she pulled each ankle up to her hamstrings, then hugged her knee to her chest. Lucas wouldn't mind having her hug his head to her chest, either. He wished he could call out and go with her, but...

"See, now, this is where I get tripped up," Kieran said.

Seeing his father's lagging upper-body strength, he made a mental note to have him work with heavier weights on his good arm. "Don't overcompensate by leaning into your strong side. Try to distribute your weight evenly."

"Hi, Lucas!" Jocelyn called out. "Hi, Mr. Grady!"

"Call me Kieran, would you?" The man had perfected the scowl.

No wonder she didn't come their way; instead she waved and headed off down the street. Lucas watched, remembering how he couldn't get her out of his mind last night. He could definitely get used to kissing Jocelyn on a regular basis.

Her narrow hips swayed rhythmically with each stride. He knew if she headed north, she'd take the route they'd run the other night. But she headed south today, so she was probably going over to the park and into the cross-country trails, the same ones the school track team used for longer runs. He remembered that Jocelyn liked routine, and she probably knew exactly how many miles she'd clock today. Yeah, she was heading to the cross-country trails. Too bad he couldn't go with her.

"Whoa, whoa, w'oh!"

Just in time, Lucas glanced back at his father, off balance and on his way down. He bolted for him. "I got you!" It took all his strength, but Lucas was damned if he was going to let his father hit the pavement because he'd been ogling his next-door neighbor. Even if it was Jocelyn Howard.

Jocelyn took the steady incline of the jogging path with precision. First one foot then the other, focused, charged with energy, up she went. She'd loved the Gandyville five-mile cross-country path since she'd first run it in high school. This morning it was the perfect distraction from thinking about Lucas Grady.

How could she not think about him? Last night, she'd carelessly thrown herself into his arms and kissed him with the passion she'd been bottling up since she'd first seen Leo kiss Kate in *Titanic*. Sure, she'd had a good reason: They'd earned $15,000 for the track program and could buy new and badly needed sports equipment, not to mention replace the threadbare maroon and gold track and warm-up uniforms. All their hard work had paid off, and she'd done it! She hadn't screwed up. Somehow, everything had fallen into place and the event had been a huge success. A few anonymous "angel" donations had helped propel them to the goal. And success felt sweet.

So had the kiss.

Thinking about locking lips with Lucas made her cheeks warm. She took a swig of water from the bottle hanging at her waist, then hit the challenge of the next incline with added vigor. Thinking about Lucas and last night's kiss, she had a lot of excess energy to work off today.

That kiss. It'd felt hard and soft all at once. And thrilling. She'd tingled in places she never thought could tingle. In front of God and practically the entire school, she'd catapulted into his arms and laid one on him, finally touching him, tasting him, and the amazing thing was…he'd kissed her back. Unlike that little peck on the lips the other night, this kiss had zinged right down to her toes.

Had she ever come close to being this charged and lit up after kissing Rick?

She fished out her cell phone and checked how long she'd been running. Not nearly long enough. This victory lap needed to be long and consuming. She needed to wear herself out so that all of her energy got zapped, and it would take every ounce of concentration to get her mind off her sore muscles, or she'd never be able to stop thinking about Lucas Grady today.

With her face burning and thighs tingling, she pressed on, up and over the small hill. On the steep downside in the middle of the path, her shoe grazed and slid off a rock, twisting her foot and sending a sharp burn up her ankle. Off balance, her arms thrashed and sliced the air on a forward lunge. As if in slow motion, she swam along, helpless to stop the fall. Her cell phone slipped through her fingers and launched into the air.

She felt her palms hit the sharp gravel first, stinging but breaking the fall. Next her chin and right shoulder crashed down. Air pushed from her lungs, making an oomph sound. Her knees struck the ground with a thud, small pebbles slicing into the skin, shin bones grinding the earth when she landed. She rolled down the path, her right side taking the brunt of the fall. The burn in her ankle seared up her leg. Several points of pain made themselves known as she lay stunned, flat on her back, the wind knocked out of her.

After a few moments, recovering her breath and beginning to put her thoughts back together, she lifted and examined her shredded palms. Raising her head, she saw bleeding knees and could tell that swelling had already set in. She slowly rotated her tight and thickening ankle and, though it hurt like hell, gratefully realized that it probably wasn't broken. After glancing again at her mangled knees, she dropped her head back on the ground with a groan.

"Crap!"

A faint beep-beep-beep in the distance let her know she'd received a text message. The sound seemed to come from the ravine over by a tree—where her cell phone had landed.

Now what?

Lucas tapped on Jocelyn's front door with a lame excuse. His mother was so thrilled to have her cast off, she'd made a huge Tex-Mex lunch and insisted he invite Jocelyn over to celebrate last night's success. He saw the gesture for what it was—blatant matchmaking— and where he may have protested in the past, today he was actually grateful. He couldn't get her out of his mind, so the thought of spending extra time with her had a certain appeal.

He'd called over the fence first but hadn't gotten a response. He'd texted her, too. Now he knocked on the front door again, and when no one came, he looked through the garage window and saw her car. It occurred to him she might still be running.

Two hours? That was a heck of a long run, even for her. A thread of worry twined through his mind and he made a snap decision.

He ran back inside his house long enough to put on his jogging shoes and grab the car keys. "Mom, hold off on lunch. Jocelyn's missing and I'm going to find her."

Several minutes later he parked at the base of Gandyville and cut the car engine. He'd never forgotten the well-worn and grueling cross-country path where his father used to regularly take the team. In those days,

Coach Dad had run along with them, and often faster than his students.

Lucas couldn't know for sure if this was where Jocelyn had come, but his gut told him to check here first. A couple other cars were in the lot, and he knew hikers and off-road cyclists also enjoyed the hills. Maybe they'd seen her.

All he could hope for was that if Jocelyn were here, she'd stayed on the old path. Otherwise, he didn't have a clue how to find her.

He'd kept his eye out for her on the drive over but hadn't seen any runners. This was his only plan, and he could make a huge fool out of himself scouring the hills for nothing. Maybe she was already home. Maybe she'd been in the shower when he knocked on the door. For all he knew she could be having lunch with a friend. He tried her cell phone one last time. No answer.

He got out of the car, not bothering to warm up, and hit the beginning of the trail loop.

Jocelyn rolled onto her knees, paying the price with a surge in pain and stinging. After wrangling with balance and more pain, she managed to stand on her one good leg. She hopped across the path and fell against a tree, hoping to spot her cell phone. No such luck. By her estimation she was half a mile out from the end of the trail. She shaded her eyes and scanned the nearby hills. No one seemed to be around. In the distance she spotted a hiker or two, but they were too far away to hear her if she called out. She took the chance and tried anyway.

"Hello! Help! I'm over here!" Nothing. She took a swig of water from her waist pack to quench her dried throat and tried again. "Hello!"

She hopped from under the tree to a large boulder on the other side of the path. The view from this direction didn't produce any hikers or bicyclists, either. Where was everyone today?

She tested putting weight on her foot. A hot poker seared up the inside of her calf. It felt like a sprained ankle. Then she hopped to the next rock. The burst of Latin samba drums and whistles alerted her to her phone ringing. It sounded nearby…in the ditch. Nope, she'd resist the temptation of going after it, instead memorizing the tree and planning to come back at another time for the phone. She'd hop and limp her way back down the path until she found somebody to help her.

Lucas tucked his cell phone in his T-shirt pocket when he came to the fork in the trail. Jocelyn still wasn't answering. He took off running, eyes sweeping every nook and crevice for her. He thought about cupping his hands around his mouth and shouting her name but decided to hold off for now. On he went, and after a sharp turn he spotted her a couple hundred yards out. The rush of relief almost knocked him off balance. He stabilized himself, rushing onward.

"Hey!" he yelled at Jocelyn hobbling down the path. What the hell?

"Lucas!" She stopped and leaned against a rock.

He sprinted toward her, his pulse pounding in his ears. Coming close, she didn't need to explain what had happened; her bloody knees and messed-up ankle told the story. She'd obviously taken a header.

"When you weren't home, I took a chance on the old cross-country path," he said when he finally reached her, breathless and happy as hell he'd listened to his gut instinct. He assessed her head to foot, noting her injuries. "Man, you're a mess."

"I know."

"Want to explain what you were doing out here all by yourself without a cell phone?"

"Cell's in a ditch back there," Jocelyn answered. He looked behind her, contemplating looking for it. He was game, but she shook her head. "I just want to go home."

"Tell you what, you can explain everything later. Let's get you home so I can clean you up," he said, having no intention of letting her lean on him and limp the rest of the way to the parking lot. Instead, he swooped in and scooped her up without protest and headed down the path toward the car with her secure in his arms.

Chapter Seven

Jocelyn's protests went unheard. Lucas would have nothing to do with her limping her way into the house. He'd parked in her driveway and picked her up from the passenger seat, carrying her like a newlywed toward the bridal suite. Locked in the cradle of his strength, she almost forgot her ankle hurt like hell.

"This isn't necessary. You'll injure yourself," she said.

"I've carried two-hundred-pound soldiers over my shoulders. You're skinny. Now shut up and get out the house key."

Nestled close against him, she caught the scent of soap tamped down by the hours of the day. Lingering hints of aftershave, with just enough effects from the sun mixed in from looking for her, gave him a total "guy smell."

He'd searched for her and had come to her rescue—how romantic was that? She wanted to nuzzle her face into his neck, but that was a bad idea. Anyhow, he'd given her a simple assignment—unlock the door.

She fished inside the waist pack as Lucas lowered her just enough to put her even with the lock. It was as if doing arm curls at the gym, and his strength surprised her. Lucas wasn't bulky like Rick had become; he was naturally strong with muscles earned from hard work—not by spending time with barbells. She'd noticed that long before today, and she really liked what she saw. And now, she definitely liked how it felt.

As she unlocked the door and he brought her inside, she tried not to fantasize about the significance of being carried over the threshold. Again, something much more exciting than a sprained ankle came to mind. What would it be like if…

He plopped her onto the couch, abruptly bringing her mind back to the present. "Thanks!"

Without asking, he lifted her injured leg and propped it up on two throw pillows, then headed to her kitchen. "Do you have an ice pack?"

"Yes. In the freezer."

"How about a bandage?"

"In the front bathroom, under the vanity. I keep a first aid kit there."

He closed the refrigerator like a typical guy, hard and loud. Then she heard drawers open and close and other cupboards clunked closed. What was he doing—making her lunch?

Lucas reappeared with a tall glass of water in one hand and the ice pack wrapped in a dishtowel in the other. "Here you go." He handed her the water, then gingerly placed the ice on her propped-up ankle. "I found aspirin so I brought you a couple." He dug into his T-shirt pocket and fished out two little pills. She took them as he headed off down the hall toward the front bathroom.

Through the distortion of the glass she watched him, enjoying the purposeful moves of a man on task. She lowered the glass to watch his broad shoulders and really cute rear end. Halfway down the hall he popped into the guest bedroom. She stretched her neck to keep him in her line of vision. Soon, he reemerged with a pillow, then continued down the hall for the first aid kit. A few seconds later, he placed a soft pillow behind her head.

"How's that?"

"Great, but you don't have to wait on…"

He shut her up with an index finger placed softly over her lips. Yikes, that stopped her from speaking, but it also had her wanting to shock him by sucking on it. What in the world was she thinking? Her ankle hurt like she'd been kicked by a horse, her knees burned and her palms ached. Not exactly the right setting for a girl to think those kinds of thoughts, but Lucas looking after her made the fine hair on her neck stand up, and, well, he was so darn close…and there was that tart trace of aftershave again.

"First," he said, "I'm going to wrap this ankle before it has the chance to swell any more." He removed her shoe, opened the cloth bandage and gently put her ankle through range of motion before rolling the stretchy bandage around her injury.

"It's not broken," she said, hoping her foot didn't smell after her long run, yet knowing the odds were against all hope. At least she'd had a pedicure last week.

"Nope. Doesn't look like it. Wiggle your toes for me."

She did, and he smiled. What she'd give to read his mind.

She glanced over the abrasions on her legs and back at Lucas. "Dude, I'm mangled."

"Totally thrashed, Joss." He smiled again, as if he were proud of her road rash.

She enjoyed watching his long fingers and strong hands do the simplest of tasks. For a guy who regularly worked on his classic car, his hands and fingernails were clean and well cared for. She put her head back on the pillow and stared at the ceiling to help get her mind off the many ways she adored Lucas. She'd be setting herself up for big disappointment going down that path. He didn't want to be back in Whispering Oaks any more than his sister Anne had. Why couldn't they see the beauty of their hometown and making a life here? Was there something wrong with her for wanting to stay and be the best teacher she could be?

"There you go," Lucas said, finishing the wrap by lightly patting her calf before putting the ice pack back in place.

The touch took her right out of her thoughts and back into his hazel eyes. "Thanks."

"No worries. Now, I'll need a basin and a washcloth."

Her head came off the pillow as she drew her brows together. "You don't need…"

There went the finger on the lips again. This time she snapped at it and he yanked his finger away with a playful nod and an unidentifiable glint in those yummy eyes. "Let me remind you that you're at a serious disadvantage."

She tried to sock his arm but missed. *Go ahead. Take advantage. I'm okay with that.* "All the stuff you need is in that front bathroom."

"You should be grateful," he said, swaggering away.

Oh, she was grateful, all right. "That you saved the day? Thanks. But hey, I would have made it home somehow."

"I know 'cause you're the can-do girl, right?"

Right.

Within a couple of minutes he sat on the coffee table next to the couch with warm water in a basin and plain white soap. She bit her bottom lip in anticipation of soap irritating her already-burning knees.

"I promise to be gentle." He nailed her with those heavy-lidded hazel-green eyes and all concerns left her mind while she became a puddle of cooperation. As he dipped the washcloth into the water, she couldn't avoid staring at his mouth—the deep, pinky-width groove on his upper lip, how kissable it was.

He moved toward her and with his thumb and middle finger lifted her face. Anticipation rushed through her like a hidden spring. "I noticed you scraped your chin, too."

He'd been blessed with a full lower lip that rested above his angular chin and begged to be kissed.

And she wanted to, right now. "Ouch!"

"Sorry if it burns, but we've got to clean up your cuts." He dabbed at the abrasion under her chin with soap and water. "You don't want to get an infection on top of everything else, right?" His eyes concentrated on the task, not her. All she could do was think about their kiss the other night and how much she wanted to do it again. Soon!

"Right," she mimicked.

"You've got some deep gashes on your knees." He moved out from the close proximity as if sensing her reaction to the intimate act of washing her chin. Did she have any effect on him?

"Gee, you think?" She covered her eyes with her hands, more to help her quit staring at his sexy mouth than out of any cowardly need. "I don't want to watch."

"Don't be wussy." He patted her thigh, and she quickly lost track of what she was worried about.

He finished the job of cleaning her cuts, skillfully washing each knee in turn and being surprisingly gentle about it, with not a clumsy bone in his hands. It stung, but for some reason she didn't mind. He pulled one hand away from her eyes. "This needs cleaning, too." Damn, his mouth was right in her eyeshot again as he pulled her palms toward him to examine them.

He ended the cleaning by fishing out some antibiotic ointment and dabbing it on her knees, then covering them with gauze and tape. Large square Band-Aids worked for her palms. Last he used a cotton swab to put the ointment on her chin. He dabbed away as she looked at him. Concentrating on the task, his soft breath tickled her neck. He lifted his head, eyes directly in line with hers. His irises had tiny brown and gold flecks in them and a dark outline around the cornea. Those gorgeous eyes also made her want to kiss him—everything about him. from the part in his hair to the small cut on his thumb, made her want to kiss him—and the goose bumps running down her arms were probably a dead giveaway.

Something subtle in his gaze suggested he might be interested in kissing her, too.

Should she make a move? Couldn't she call it a thank-you kiss?

"Lucas! Jocelyn!" Beverly called through the screen because Lucas hadn't closed the door on their way in. "Is everything okay?"

"Hey, Mom." Lucas jumped to attention, letting his mother inside. She'd come with two aluminum-foil-wrapped plates of food that smelled like melted cheese and spices—in other words, heavenly, though food was the last thing on Jocelyn's mind. As disappointment set in that in her perfect-world fantasy Lucas may have considered kissing her again but had gotten waylaid by his well-meaning mother, Jocelyn tried to look cheery for Mrs. Grady.

"Oh, honey, are you all right?"

"Thanks to your son, I'll be just fine."

"I was giving her a lecture on the buddy system and how she shouldn't be running alone on those cross-country trails," he said, a mischievous glint in his gaze encouraging her to play along.

"You've got a point," Beverly said. "Good thing Lucas went looking for you. Oh, my God, he was so worried he—"

"Mom." He cut her off.

Beverly got the point. "You probably shouldn't stay alone tonight, either. Lucas, she's probably all shook up, so why don't you camp out on her couch?"

All shook up was an understatement, but it had more to do with Lucas than the fall.

The thought of Lucas Grady sleeping under the same roof with her had definite appeal, and it made the backs of her knees tingle. Right on, Beverly! *I like your plan.*

After they ate the lunch of southwest chicken enchiladas and rice Mom had brought over, Lucas made a point to keep a safe distance from Jocelyn. She looked so damn vulnerable laid up on the couch and, well, he'd come way too close to kissing her before Mom barged in.

He sat in the recliner near the sofa as they watched Jocelyn's favorite movie, *Gladiator*. He'd expected her comfort movie would be a chick flick and was surprised when she suggested this one. But Jocelyn was never like the other girls growing up. His sisters were definitely girly-girls, but Jocelyn was fine with whatever. He liked that about her.

Glancing at her dozing off, brown lashes brushing her lower lids, he decided he still liked that she was a "whatever" kind of girl. Well, now a woman. Her lashes fluttered open. Could she feel him watching her?

"I've got to use the bathroom," she said.

"Okay. Let me help you down there."

Jocelyn sat up, making a grimace, obviously remembering how sore she was. He helped her stand and tucked her close to his waist on the injured side so she could hop along beside him. He'd gotten the impression earlier she didn't like him carrying her everywhere, though he kind of dug it.

Once she was delivered into the bathroom he waited outside, giving her enough space for privacy.

"Lucas?" she called through the door.

Already? "Yeah."

"I just remembered I have an old pair of crutches in the attic. Maybe you can get them down, so I won't have to be so dependent on you?"

He kind of liked having her dependent on him, but he also understood it wasn't her style. "Good idea. I'll check it out right now."

Lucas went to the upstairs hallway and glanced upward at the ceiling trapdoor to the attic. He gave the string a tug, pulled down the attached ladder and made his way into the attic. He quickly found the metal crutches leaning in the corner. They'd need some cleaning up but they were good enough. On his way to get them he noticed an old dresser covered in the track trophies Jocelyn had won back in high school. One had a framed picture with it. The photograph was of the two of them in eleventh grade, all lanky and knobby kneed but grinning wide. It brought back a memory of the semester she'd talked him into training with her, and he'd won a trophy for most improved athlete at the end of year track banquet. He couldn't remember who seemed prouder, Jocelyn or his parents.

"I'm done!" she called, and he jumped out of memory lane and down the attic ladder and stairs with the crutches in tow to help her back down the hall.

The evening went on in comfortable companionship. He walked her dogs, Diesel and Daisy, while she napped. He cleaned and adjusted the old crutches, then helped her practice walking with them. He fed the dogs for her, and when she gave the okay, he let them into the house. They watched another DVD, a so-so comedy. Bored, he started talking over it.

"I saw all of your trophies in the attic."

"Oh, those. Mom refuses to get rid of them."

"Saw a funny picture of you and me holding our trophies, too."

She made a funny face, eyes wide, as if she'd been caught with a big secret. "Can you believe how skinny I was?"

"Hey, me, too." He cleared his throat, patted the Lab's

head, then when the golden retriever pushed his head in between him and the other dog, he patted his head, too. "I, uh, wouldn't have ever won a single trophy if it wasn't for you. Don't suppose I ever thanked you."

"Hey." She came up on her elbow and looked at him. "You let me get a picture with you. That made my day!"

He shook his head, not understanding what she'd ever seen in him. He'd been nothing but a pain in the butt, disrespectful and a know-it-all back then, yet she'd still liked him. Adored him, even.

"I've been thinking," he said.

"Yeah?" The dogs were now poking their noses everywhere, making themselves pests. She smiled at both of them, and he liked how her eyes curved upward.

"I think you should go for the head coach job at Whispering Oaks."

"Are you kidding? That's your father's job."

"Dad is getting up in years, and after that awful accident, the truth is he knows he won't ever be the same. He was just grousing about all the responsibility of running track this morning. I'm thinking if you take the angle of letting him know you're interested in taking over head coach, he might not feel obligated to continue in the position. It might give him an out, you know?"

"That's devious!"

"No, it isn't. It's communicating with him and letting him know you're interested in the job. It would be devious to apply behind his back."

She flopped back on the couch. "I'd never do that. I know you think I'm so 'can-do,' but it's too much for me, Lucas. I've barely survived, and now with this sprain, how am I going to finish the year?"

"You'll find a way. Remember, you really are the can-do girl. What's the word my dad always uses? Delegate. Assign more responsibility to the other coaches."

"Why can't your dad do that, too?" She was back up on her elbow again, looking battered and cute with her ponytail all askew and flopping in her face.

"Believe me, he will. And it bothers the hell out of him not to do everything he used to. What I'm saying is maybe it's time for the track team to have someone new. Someone like you, who gets excited and is totally supportive of the kids."

"Your dad does that."

"New blood. Like you."

"What would your dad do?"

"He can be the hurdle coach. Or your assistant. Look, I'm sure he'd be happy to stay in the classroom and give up running the whole show. Just think about it, is all I'm saying."

She lay back down and stared at the ceiling. Both dogs sniffed around her head as she thought. Daisy licked her cheek. "I really don't want to make your dad upset, but I promise to think about what you've said. After I do, I'll talk to him about it. See how he really feels."

"All right." He patted her shoulder and turned the volume back up on the movie. "You need anything?"

"There're some cookies in the cupboard. Will you bring me a couple?"

Not only did he bring her the cookies but ice cream, too. He liked how she turned the spoon backward and licked off the ice cream like a lollipop. Maybe he should give her ice cream more often.

They finished watching the movie and found nothing good to watch on TV.

"I should probably go to bed," she said.

"Let me get you a couple more aspirin so you won't be achy tonight."

"Thanks." She gave him a look that said a lot more than thanks, and he looked away because he liked how it felt. He liked being here with her, doing little things that she appreciated, and he loved how her grateful glances spread over him like melting butter. He liked how he could be as quiet as he wanted or talk—either seemed to be okay with her. He liked looking at her legs, even though they were all banged up. Hell, he liked having an excellent excuse to look at them, too.

He brought her the aspirin and sat on the edge of the couch, handing her the water. She took and swallowed them and returned the glass, wiping her mouth with the back of her hand. He made sure her bandages were all in place.

"Seriously, I don't know what I would have done today without your help." She touched his arm, sincerity pouring out of her soft brown eyes.

"Hey, that's what friends are for, right?"

She sat up, her cool hands cupping his cheeks. "Thank you, for everything."

He was pretty sure she pulled him closer, but he

didn't need to be encouraged. His lips were heading right for her mouth and nothing, not even his mother calling at the front door, was going to stop him this time.

He kissed her gently at first. Making contact with her lips sent a sweet warm ripple over his chin and down his neck. He helped her lay her head back on the pillow. He kept kissing her while she wrapped her arms around his neck, and once he felt the tip of her tongue on the crease of his lips, he angled his head and kissed her deeper. She tasted like warm mint-chip ice cream.

She surprised him by nibbling and tugging on his bottom lip, which revved him up and released a satisfying wave of heat down his center. The kisses got messy, sounds were emitted, heads turned and repositioned, fingers dug into hair and tongues touched and darted, imitating something far more intimate than kissing.

He wrapped his arm around her back and let the other hand roam over her side and hips, enjoying the solid feel of her, moving back up, finding her breast and finally exploring the body he'd been so fascinated with lately. She didn't disappoint. Soft breast, just enough for his palm, warmed him up and turned him on. When he slipped his fingers beneath her sports bra, she didn't stop him, instead encouraging him with a moan. Her breast was tight and the nipple erect and all he could think about was putting it in his mouth. He did. Sweet mercy. She whimpered and arched and he realized her nipple wasn't the only thing erect.

He wanted to undress her right here, dive into her

body and explore every inch of her. But most of all, he wanted to be on top of her, to feel her beneath him, and he shifted his position on the couch, threw his leg over her then crawled on top.

"Ouch!" she yelped.

Oh, damn. So lost in the make-out session, he'd forgotten about her banged-up knees and swollen ankle. "I'm sorry." He rolled off and stood up. "I totally forgot."

With her hair a mess, lips puffy and pink from their shared kisses and one perky breast on display, Jocelyn smiled up at him. "Give me a couple of days?"

"I totally took advantage of you, Jocelyn. I'm sorry."

She cocked her head and made an indignant expression. "I'm not."

Chapter Eight

Lucas stood in the shower letting water pour over his head and face. If he were smart he'd turn the temperature down to cold. He'd hardly slept at all last night, preferring to stay on the couch at Jocelyn's house, keeping the dogs company as he quietly clicked through the TV cable channels.

What if he'd fallen asleep and had one of his nightmares? What if he'd woken up yelling and sweating and scaring the hell out of Jocelyn? That was the last thing he ever wanted to do. The one and only time it'd happened since he got home, his mother practically had a heart attack thinking someone had broken into the house. When he explained that sometimes he still had battle dreams, she looked so freakin' worried he wanted to puke.

He turned, rested his forehead against the cold tile and let the water pelt his back. Man, Jocelyn knew how to get him all worked up with her kisses. He shook his head. What the hell was he supposed to do about that? He grabbed a bar of soap and lathered his shoulders, which made him think about his raven tattoos. Where the hell were Hugin and Munin last night? He'd needed his brains and reason then. Jocelyn was the kind of girl a guy got involved with, not a hit-and-run encounter. He had no business messing with her like that, but man... that girl knew how to kiss.

He'd made her a pot of coffee when he first heard her stir upstairs early that morning, calling out, "You okay?" when she got into the shower.

"I'm fine. Thanks!" she'd answered in her usual cheery voice, leaving him with all kinds of steamy images of her naked and wet.

He'd waited to make sure she'd gotten out okay, when he knew she was getting dressed.

"I'll see you, then." And he was out of there. He had to leave or he'd be breaking down her bedroom door.

Coward.

He scrubbed his chest and pits with soap. He may as well be honest about it—he was a relationship coward. If you looked at dating as a barter system, which he tended to do, each party was supposed to bring something to the table. She brought looks, personality and a good job. He could only bring a messed-up mind, a stubborn streak and unemployment. Oh yeah, he was a real prize.

After what Joss had gone through with that loser ex-fiancé of hers, the last thing she needed was a guy like Lucas.

He stepped out of the shower and dried off, resolved to avoid Jocelyn and do anything but get involved with her. It was for her own good. She didn't need a guy like him messing with her mind. She had enough going on these days.

Frustrated, he dried his hair, rubbing too damn hard and nearly giving his scalp rug burn. He'd keep busy, help his dad as usual and then spend the rest of the day working on the car. Installing upholstery was best left to experts, but he was determined to do it himself. Worst case scenario—he'd have to buy new seats. In the meantime, keeping busy nonstop might help him sleep tonight. He definitely needed a good night's sleep.

As tired as he was by nightfall, he hardly slept Sunday night or Monday. Jocelyn kept flickering on the edge…along with something far more sinister.

Tuesday afternoon, Lucas tinkered on the Mustang in the garage with heavy metal music blasting from the tinny old radio. He'd reinstalled the bucket seats and now sat on a low stool and waxed the new paint job, getting lost in the routine.

"Hi."

He turned to find Jocelyn balanced on her crutches, dressed as if she'd just gotten home from teaching.

Dark gray slacks covered her injured knees and swollen ankle. She wore a pale gray tank top with a sleeveless sweater and some kind of necklace with big bobble beads. Her arms looked tan and buff holding her up on the crutches, and she'd pulled her hair back into that signature ponytail that swayed when she walked. As if a bucket of blood had been dumped into his gut, he felt the color drain from his face, and he had to make a quick recovery.

"Hey," he said like nothing bothered him in the universe, especially not the sight of Jocelyn.

She smiled, and though partially shaded, her eyes were bright. She came closer, leaned against the car and tapped him with one of the crutches. "It's been a couple of days."

It would have been a lot more if he'd had his way. It had been awkward enough when he had to borrow her van to take Dad for his final cast appointment yesterday. She'd known exactly what he needed and had silently handed him the keys.

"How are those knees and that ankle getting along?"

"I'm doing much better. Thanks." She must have read his body language because she didn't look nearly as playful now as when she'd arrived. He needed to keep everything between them superficial. It was the right thing to do, even though he hated the idea of jacking her around.

"Good. You come to talk to my father about the job?"

She crinkled her nose. "I'm not ready to do that yet."

"Ah, come on, tell him straight up." He sounded impatient, gruffer than he'd intended, but he'd hardly slept for days now and he was edgy with exhaustion.

"That's easy for you to say, Lucas." The last thing he needed was a challenge.

"Easy for me? Nothing's easy for me these days." He threw the rag on the counter and walked toward her. "I can't sleep. I'm fed up with Mom and Dad hinting I need to start thinking about the future. I don't give a flying…"

"You don't have to figure everything out right now. Just concentrate on getting back into a routine."

He leaned both hands on the car and nailed her with an aggravated stare. "And I don't need you telling me what to do, either." He expected her to crumple, but he'd forgotten who he was dealing with—Little Miss Cheerleader. Crap.

She put her free hand on her hip and tossed him another challenging glance. "Quit being a pill. Get over yourself, dude."

Nearby, a passing motorcycle backfired. It jolted Lucas right down to the nerve endings on the soles of his feet. He grabbed the counter, fight and flight simultaneously kicking in, adrenaline pouring into his chest. He let the F-word fly…a half-dozen times. It was like the track meet all over again. Would this ever end? Grinding his molars, he forced himself to stay perfectly still while his pulse thundered between his ears.

"Are you okay?" He saw the concern in her eyes, the worry. He didn't need her pity. No way in hell would he let her pity him.

Glaring at her, he strode past close enough to brush her shoulder. She flinched. Steaming full speed ahead, he lunged toward the unfinished garage wall, and between two planks of wood he did his damn best to ram his fist through the insulation padding. Thwap! It took three good punches to break through. When the ringing in his ears stopped and the stinging in his knuckles brought him back to the present, he glanced first at the hole in the wall, then at Jocelyn. She stood stock-still, as if incapable of moving, alarm radiating from her eyes.

He hated that look, and he'd put it there.

Damn it all to hell, he'd frightened the crap out of her. He wanted to punch the wall again but forced control. "I'm sorry, Joss." He moderated his tone, sounding dead, flat and obligatory. "I didn't mean to scare you."

Clamping her lips tight, she recoiled when he took a step toward her. It made him queasy. "I'd never hurt you, Jocelyn. I swear. I'd never hit a woman."

Her chin quivered, and he saw a battle inside her as she must have tried to make sense of his outburst. "I know you wouldn't. I've just never seen you like that before."

"Look, I told you this PTSD crap is a bitch. I'm not the guy I used to be. You can't say I haven't warned you."

"I understand." By the expression on her face, she looked anything but understanding. She still looked scared as hell.

Silence ruled the moments as he licked and bit his lips and tried to make eye contact with her again. She avoided his gaze, chewing the corner of her mouth. "Have you thought about therapy? Don't they have groups of soldiers with the same problem where you can talk about it? Where they understand?"

He nodded, tired of the same old advice, over and over. *Been there. Done that. Didn't come close to feeling better.*

He wanted to touch her, help her know his hands would always be kind to her. But when he took a step closer she got skittish and clutched her crutches as if preparing to take off—or to use them as defense. It broke his heart.

The damage had been done. He'd managed to alienate the one person who'd always believed in him besides his sister Anne.

"Well, uh, I just wanted to say hi and make sure you hadn't fallen off the planet, you know?" Her eyes shone as moisture gathered. "I've missed you," she said as she took off on her crutches and headed for home. "See you around," she said scurrying down the driveway.

Great going, loser. You screwed up again. Maybe he *should* fall off the planet.

What did it matter? He was no good for anyone. Maybe this was for the best. He didn't know who he was anymore or what he wanted to do. Or where he belonged. Maybe he should reenlist. Civilian life wasn't going too well.

He rubbed his aching fist, realizing he'd drawn blood. What could Jocelyn possibly want with him, anyway?

* * *

Jocelyn couldn't get home fast enough. Wasn't that exactly what had happened with Rick—he'd simply turned into someone else? Did she need to learn that lesson more than once? Her heart still thumped in her chest as she fumbled with the crutches to go faster, hoping she didn't stumble.

Lucas wasn't the guy he used to be. She'd seen him lose it when he was a teenager, but she'd never feared him. Until today. Maybe it was because of Rick, but just now when he'd put his fist through the wall, and with that panicked angry stare he'd leveled at her, Lucas made her tremble—as if he wanted her to—and she'd promised she'd never put herself in that position again.

I'm not the guy I used to be. You can't say I haven't warned you.

She wouldn't have to be warned again.

Once inside the house and, because something in her gut insisted she not let it go just yet, she went directly to the computer. She might have a pile of anatomy pop quizzes to grade and a midterm to organize, but first she intended to do some research on PTSD.

A half hour later she slumped back in her office chair, head full of statistics about an enormous problem. Anywhere from 6 percent to 20 percent of soldiers from Iraq and Afghanistan returned home with some form of PTSD. How could they be helped? Right there in writing, an article said it: just listen. She'd done that the other night when they'd taken a run together and Lucas seemed to open up, relax some. So that was a good start. But then she read the next two sentences out loud.

"Don't try to fix your vet. The military trains soldiers to be strong and self-sufficient. Asking for help goes against their training." Great, that's exactly what she'd just done—offered a snap fix, suggested he try therapy. Farther down the article she read, "Someone who's always cheerful can be annoying to a returning soldier." Oh, God, she was a hopeless cheerleader. Always had been. Didn't Lucas even call her the can-do girl the other day? He'd probably meant it as a snide remark.

As she finished the article, "Helping the Soldiers You Love," one last encouraging item caught her attention. "With the support of family and friends, wartime stress eases over time. For those who don't get better, get help. It's out there. However, for the newly returning soldier, sometimes the best PTSD therapy is B + Double S + Triple F—beer + sex + sleep + favorite fast food."

She gave a tension-relieving smile as hope sparked in her chest. Having a better understanding of PTSD made his outburst less scary.

A mischievous thought involving beer and pizza twined through her mind. Well, what do you know? Maybe she could help him put the BSSFFF method into action.

Having moved aside the family room furniture to make space for Dad's daily workout, father and son did the daily routine.

"Two more sets. Come on." Lucas tolerated the

death glare from his father, knowing the man would do anything to get some strength back in his leg. To be independent again. Bart stuck his head in between Lucas and Kieran, no doubt to make sure everything was under control. Dad offered him a benign pat, and when Bart turned to check out Lucas, he sniffed the dog right back, nose to nose. Bart liked that.

The cast had finally come off. Hallelujah. Now Kieran had a lot of work to do to get his muscles back to normal.

"This is exactly what the physical therapist said to do." Lucas led his father, who was lying on a throw rug over the wood floors, through range of motion, bending and straightening his knee, turning his foot round and round at the ankle, lifting and lowering the leg.

"Well, you know what, son?" Kieran grunted. "You'd make a great P.T. technician. Ever think about torturing people for a living?" he said, face in a grimace while he pushed against Lucas's hands.

"You're not serious, right?" The difference in muscle mass between the casted leg and the other was extreme. How could a leg atrophy that much in eight weeks? Not to mention look this dried up and scaly.

"Maybe. You've got to think about doing something. Unless you're planning to live with us the rest of your life, and, well, I've got some news for you…"

"Don't worry. I'm not sticking around much longer."

When Kieran finished the last set of exercises, and proved he still knew how to balance himself without crutches, Lucas made both of them lunch. Bart happily followed along, hoping that one of them would accidentally on purpose drop food on the floor.

"I'm going to work on the car," Lucas said. "Want to keep me company?"

"Sure. Now that your mom's back teaching I'd get lonely without you around."

He smiled at his dad and saw sincerity in his eyes. Somehow, with their rocky relationship, they'd settled into a comfortable bond over the past several weeks. As they headed out the back door, with Kieran walking a bit gingerly trying out his leg, Lucas pat his father's back.

"I'll race you!" Kieran said.

Twenty minutes later, both men sipped sodas from the garage mini refrigerator. Kieran was sprawled out on a chaise lounge in the May sun at the mouth of the garage with Bart by his side contentedly soaking up the rays. Lucas got out the newly arrived vintage 1965 Mustang car grille.

"You know, at the rate you stick around Whispering Oaks, this classic car won't ever get a victory lap around town."

"Don't even think about borrowing it." He slipped the grille in place, admired the mint condition and went about securing it.

"Not enough leg space for a man my size."

"What's up with that, anyway? How come you're six-four and I never made it past six-one?"

"Blame it on your mother. She's the short side of the family."

"I never wanted to go out for basketball, anyway."

"What *did* you want to do? I know I always pushed you into going to college, but…"

"Honestly? I think I wanted to be an auto mechanic. Maybe an auto-body technician. I knew that disappointed you, Dad, but I'm just being honest here, since you asked."

"Then I'll be honest, too. I was adamantly opposed to you enlisting instead of going to college."

Lucas tapped the small wrench in the air. "That was very apparent."

Dad gave a chagrined smile. "Yeah, I get it. Well, I've come to understand that we all have different paths. Not everyone is ready for college right out of high school."

"Thank you! Finally, I make my point."

"Okay, don't rub it in, but that was then, this is now. Since you've been home, you've been a great help, and your mother and I are truly grateful." His dad paused. "Now, I don't want to lecture by saying maybe it's time to explore college. But you've got the GI Bill to help pay for it. You've obviously got the brains. Add that with life experience. Man, you're good to go."

Lucas took a step back to admire his handiwork, then glanced at his father. "You want to hear a little secret?"

"I'm all ears."

"I've already signed up for a couple of basic education courses online. I start this summer."

"That's great!" His father's happy and surprised expression nearly made Lucas laugh. The man almost blew soda bubbles out his nose.

"I'm looking into some programs Jocelyn told me about for sports medicine or maybe physician's assistant. Lots of medics go that route. And that physical therapy idea you had is a good one, too, Dad."

"Are you serious? That's fantastic."

"No guarantees. I'm just looking into things, Dad. I didn't want to say anything until I'd made up my mind, but since you're nagging me…"

"Son, my lips are sealed. I won't interfere with your decision. And you're welcome to stay here as long as you need to. You see, I've grown up some, too."

"Thanks." Lucas reached for and shook his father's hand and let the sun warm his shoulders and top of his head. Now, if he could only erase that awful scene with Jocelyn four days ago.

"One other thing." The moment they broke their grip, Kieran's finger came up in the air. "About decisions and Jocelyn? When are you going to open your eyes to see…"

"End of discussion, Dad." Suddenly the Mustang needed his undivided attention. He stepped back into the garage, feeling the air cool several degrees even as his face heated up.

"But…"

"End of discussion." Lucas had torn a page out of Coach Grady's game book. That felt kind of good, too.

After a long silence, his dad dozed off. Lucas fiddled contentedly with the car, ran into the house for the camera to take some pictures of it and thought about snapping one or two of his father all slack-jawed in the lounger but decided to be nice. Soon another hour had passed, and presently Kieran came to with a snort loud enough to send Bart out of his doggie dreams.

He scrubbed his face and repositioned his ball cap. "Well," he said, glancing at his watch. "I've got the four o'clock news to watch. Better head inside."

Lucas was sitting in the car, dealing with a stubborn latch on the glove compartment. "See you later."

No more than two minutes after his dad had gone back inside the house, Jocelyn came limping up the driveway. Lucas was still in the car, though now idling the engine. His innards tensed, and his foot accidentally pushed on the gas. The engine revved.

She carried a pizza box, and a couple of beers hanging from their plastic nooses dangled from her fingers.

"Hi, Lucas!" she said cheerfully, as if nothing had ever happened.

"Hey," he said, feeling embarrassed and mixed-up inside and trying to play down her arrival. He cut the engine and hopped out of the car.

"I need to ask you a question," she said.

"Yeah? What's that?"

She wore shorts, and he could see the swelling on her sprained ankle had drastically gone down over the past week, though the bruising was a deep purple with hints of yellow. Her knees were scabbed, yet her legs still looked great. Because her tank top didn't reach her hip-hugging shorts, her midriff and flat stomach were hard to ignore. She had to know exactly what she was doing to him. His own engine revved a little.

She plopped the pizza box on the garage counter and opened it, the tomato-and-cheese aroma immediately perking up his taste buds. "Want some pizza?"

Chapter Nine

After handing Lucas a beer, Jocelyn hopped up on the garage counter, flipped around and sat. "Ouch," she said. "I forget how tight my scabs are."

Sure enough, a small drip of blood seeped from the crease of her left knee.

She opened the other can and took a quick swig, ignoring her weeping scab.

"Swelling's gone down," he pointed out, as if she hadn't known. The bandage fit snug around her ankle with bruising shooting above like purple and blue fireworks.

"Yeah, I can put some weight on it now, too."

"I noticed." He'd noticed a lot more when she'd walked up the driveway, too. Like how glad he was to see her after last time when he'd scared her and how great those shorts fit. How sweetly forgiving she'd always been with him, grinning like nothing had ever happened, and how if he tilted his head just so, he could see that patch of skin beneath her tank top.

She helped herself to the pizza and looked damn cute with three inches of mozzarella hanging from her chin as she ate. She gathered the cheese with her fingers, tilted her head and slid the strings into her mouth, taking cute to the sexy-as-hell realm. He gulped half the can of beer.

She flapped the lid of the pizza box from his favorite local Italian joint. "Come on, have a piece. You know you want to."

Did she have a clue how tempting and right-on her innocent invitation was? He hopped over the car door rather than open it and took his time walking toward Jocelyn and the pizza, a half-hitched smile tugging on his face. He wouldn't dare say what he was thinking.

Lucas took an extra-large triangle, folded it in half and shoved a third into his mouth. Man, he'd forgotten how fantastic New York–style pizza tasted, even in California. He'd made the hamburger drive-through run the first or second day he'd gotten home, but taking care of Dad had put a crimp in his eating out. "This is great," he said, mouth way too full to talk.

She smiled widely and took another bite, nailing him with a coy stare all the while.

He swallowed and narrowed his eyes. "What are you up to?"

"Can't a girl eat pizza with her next-door neighbor?" She acted all innocent, confirming his suspicions about her having something planned.

He drank more beer, took another third of the pizza slice with one bite and waited.

"So, I wanted to invite you and your parents to the last track meet of the season this Saturday."

"I knew there was a catch." He smiled, glad she'd brought him food and beer to butter him up before popping the question.

She smiled back. "Well? Will you come?"

"Of course. Just warn me before the guns go off." He grinned, then licked at the pizza sauce on the corner of his mouth.

Jocelyn watched intently. "Here's a hint." Her gaze slowly moving from his mouth to his eyes. "It happens before each race."

He connected with her steady stare for a beat or two, considering her easy solution, wondering if he really could avoid overreacting by warning himself about the starting gun.

She finished her slice, wiped her hands on her muscled and toned thighs, then jumped down. "Meet starts at ten on Saturday." She flipped the lid shut on the pizza box. "By the way, if you want more pizza, you'll have to come to my house." After picking up the box, she started to walk away. "Got more beer at my house, too."

He cocked his head, finished his beer and piece of pizza and watched her walk away, that playful ponytail swaying almost as much as her hips. She'd teased and taunted him with carbs, beer and sexual innuendo—enough to make him want more, and hell yeah, he definitely wanted more.

"Let me clean up here." He glanced around the garage wondering how quickly he could pick things up. "I'll meet you over at your house."

She didn't bother to turn around as she walked away, just waved above her head. The other day, she'd been the girl with the trembling lip and now she'd morphed into pure confidence. She was either oblivious to her actions or highly trained on how to seduce a soldier—and he had to find out which it was.

It didn't take Lucas long to holler into the house. "I'm going over to Jocelyn's." It brought him right back to his childhood when he used to play in her backyard. She was always great at imagination games and was also willing to play catch, except it was more like, let's pretend that if we miss a catch we fall into the ocean and have to dodge sharks and swim to shore. *Yeah, whatever, Joss.* He used to act like her ideas were crazy, yet he'd always go along with them because they were fun. Then again, she'd gone along with some of his wacky ideas back then, too.

As he headed toward her front steps he wondered what kind of crazy idea she had this time and why he was so willing to go along. Pizza. Beer. Joss. Sounded like a good combination to him. He whistled a tune as he took two stairs at a time.

She met him at the screen, let him in, handed him

another beer and closed and latched the door behind him. Hearing the lock click shut and seeing the serious glint in her eyes produced a light chill that tickled the back of his neck.

"Sit down."

He did. Remembering what had happened the last time he sat on her couch, he sat on the oversize chair this time and popped open his can.

She scooted off to the kitchen and brought back a paper plate with two more slices of pizza on it. He smiled and caught something sexier than pizza-serving in her eyes, which stirred him as he took a bite.

Fifteen minutes later, sated with carbs and alcohol, he was totally relaxed. He rested his head on the back of the chair and listened to a car chase in the DVD playing on her TV. When was the last time he'd felt this good? Oh, right, the last time he was here.

Without warning, Jocelyn slipped onto his lap. His head snapped up. "What're you doing?"

"Picking up where we left off." She kissed his cheek and nibbled his earlobe. That woke the nerve endings all along his chest.

"This isn't a good idea, is it?" His fingers itched to pull her ponytail free, to see her hair fall on her shoulders and feel its softness.

She kissed the side of his neck. "Let's pretend it is." She lifted her head and with huge brown eyes worked some magic that entered through his sight and made a little excursion all the way below his belt. "Let's pretend we're far, far away and it's just you and me—" she said, kissing his chin, coming ever so close to his lips but teasing away "—and there's nothing else to do…"

Okay, as bad an idea as it was, he didn't need one more word of coaxing. His arms wrapped her close and he moved in for an amazing kiss, willing and open and very inviting. He could do that—pretend nothing else mattered. Right now, kissing Jocelyn, nothing else did.

He explored her mouth and tongue, as she did the same. His hand traced up her side all the way to her breast. That's exactly where they'd left off before. Now he planned to move on to new territory. He cupped her and felt that stirring tighten low in his gut.

Her skin smelled nectar sweet as he fanned kisses over her neck and shoulder while working to remove her top. Her total cooperation made it easy to get her half naked, and man, it was well worth the effort. She was covered in goose bumps, and her small, sweet breasts got his undivided attention. As he kissed each one, she yanked and pulled off his T-shirt, forcing him to separate from those warm, velvet tips.

He looked into her dark eyes and saw a flash fire of longing. It shot through his chest, ricocheted off a few strategic places, then forged a path right down to his toes. When they hugged, with her breasts smashed tight against his chest, he understood there'd be no stopping this time. And he was ready.

"Are you sure?" he whispered over the shell of her ear.

"I've been sure about wanting to be with you since I was sixteen years old."

The sweet confession about blew off his head, and any hope for control vanished. He kissed her like he'd die if he didn't have her right that instant, and she seemed to be perfectly in sync with his flaming libido.

After greedier, nearly desperate kisses, Jocelyn broke away and pulled out her hair from the ponytail band. "Let's go," she said on a breathy rush. She jumped off his lap, and without a single thought apart from sex, he followed her down the hall and up the stairs.

Her bedroom had grown up, too. A sleek and dark wood bed covered with a brown and pink bedspread invited them to crawl on top. She stopped long enough to pull back the covers while he unzipped his jeans. She walked behind him as he checked out the satiny sheets, then heard a tiny gasp and realized she must have noticed his tattoos.

"When did you get these?" Hugging tight to his back, she kissed each shoulder.

"A couple years ago."

"They're beautiful. So powerful."

The ravens, Thought and Memory, weren't doing such a good job of keeping him on track, just now. And reason? Forget about it.

He definitely wasn't thinking when from behind she spooned against him, her warmth spreading like a soft kiss across his back, and when she slipped her hands inside his boxers every single memory in his head checked out. As she explored, it occurred to him that she enjoyed his body as much as he did her touching it, and it turned him on even more. He pivoted, his full erection pressing against her stomach. She caressed him, making every last thought, other than wanting Jocelyn and her body, fly from his head.

Somehow they made it onto the bed and he removed her shorts while kicking off his boxers, admiring all of his girl next door. Long, lean body and pert, high breasts, tight and rosy tipped. Her sexy and inviting smile melted away one yellow flag…. Things would never be the same.

It didn't matter. He covered her body with his and savored her smooth warm skin and welcoming embrace. Soon, with arms and legs wrapped and tangled tight, with tossing and rolling around the mattress, where she'd wound up on top and with hot kisses steaming up their faces, he wanted nothing more than to be inside her.

She read his mind, taking him between her thighs and pressing close. "Just a sec," she said.

In a flash she was back on top, rolling down a condom, and with the feel of her hands and fingers around him, he was ready to burst. Jumping into overdrive, they joined together, as if they couldn't breathe without the other, as if they'd belonged together for years. Moving, rocking, delving in and out. Her torso slinked along his chest as her pelvis lifted and dropped. He held her hips and dove into her like a maniac, his fire stoked by her groans and whimpers. They worked to please each other, fast, slow, long, deep and deeper. Damp with perspiration, the sweet smell of her sex drove him to the edge. He rolled on top of her, lunging deeper and faster, enjoying watching her bliss out and feeling exactly the same. She came with a gasp, and while she spasmed tightly around him he hissed air through his teeth and found release with an explosion of sensations that rattled him head to toes, until every last care got washed away.

Moments later, as the world slowly peeked back into view, he collapsed next to her, and with Jocelyn snuggled tight to his side, he slipped into a deep, sweet sleep.

One eye popped open. The bedroom had darkened as if dusk. Lucas glanced at the clock. Had he been asleep for two hours? Jocelyn was on her stomach smack to his side like a beautiful rag doll. He ran his hand along her back and over her rounded bottom, treasuring the silky feel on top and the toned muscle beneath. It stirred him.

She lifted her head and batted her lashes as she awakened. "Wow, you did me in."

"You did me, too. Don't remember when I've slept so soundly."

She got a silly look on her face and soon let go a giggle.

"What's so funny?"

"Us napping together made me think of something. Remember when we were around ten and I talked you into sleeping out back to watch the meteor showers that August?"

He grinned as a vision of yet another big idea of Jocelyn's played out, one not nearly as fun as today's. "You mean when you left me?"

"I heard coyotes, and a frog had gotten into my sleeping bag."

He grabbed and tickled her. She squirmed and laughed more. "That's no excuse for leaving me outside all night. You were such a wuss. All big ideas and no follow-through."

"I followed through today, didn't I?"

He kissed the back of her shoulder. "Big-time."

Even though he'd quit tickling her ribs, she still laughed. "If you could have seen yourself the next morning. Dead to the world." She laughed enough to make it hard to get her words out. "You were surrounded by crows and they'd broken into your popcorn."

Now he was laughing. "Oh, man. I remember I brought the popcorn so you and I could share it watching the shooting stars, which you guaranteed a million of, and I think I only saw one the whole night."

She took a deep breath, and her smile switched to a serious gaze, as if right now she saw shooting stars on him or something. The look made him want to pull her close again.

"That was so sweet," she said, now completely serious. "Bringing me popcorn."

He could only take so much of her gooey looks without wanting to jump her again. "More like dumb, if you ask me." He pinned her with an I-never-understood-how-you-could-do-it stare. "I always let you talk me into your grandiose plans. You made everything sound so great, I couldn't resist. Sleep out under the stars—" He traced her breast with his fingertips. "Just you, me and our sleeping bags." He cupped her and kissed her collarbone, then watched all the tiny chill bumps appear. He smiled. "Except there turned out to be clouds and I woke up all damp and cold from heavy dew. And you'd bailed!"

Watching her lay beside him with that adoring grin got him all worked up again.

"You loved it," she said. "Admit it."

Their eyes met and melded. "Yeah."

"And so far my grandiose pizza-and-beer plan has worked out pretty well, hasn't it?"

He pressed his hand to her belly and spread his fingers over her soft flesh. "Oh, yeah. Very impressive plan."

She kissed his chest. "Ready to admit I'm good for you?"

"Oh, you're good for me, all right." He got on his knees and lifted her up to him, and soon Jocelyn's sleek bed and mattress got another workout.

And later, after more frantic sex in the shower, he went home because the last thing he wanted his parents to think was he was screwing Jocelyn. Which of course they would think anyway, because no one went for a visit next door and stayed six hours unless hanky-panky was involved. Hot and heavy hanky-panky, the thought of which almost made him turn right around and head back for more.

How in the world was he supposed to sit on this gold mine and keep his mouth shut? Damn. Jocelyn. Who would ever have thought?

Lucas passed through the family room and waved.

"Did you have a nice time?" his mother called out.

"Yep." *Freaking fantastic monkey sex!* He'd tried his best not to make eye contact before he strolled down the hall to the room. Even so, she managed to convey she knew exactly what had gone on. With a smile.

"I'm heading for bed." As if that wasn't where he'd been all afternoon.

Just before he closed his door he swore he heard his mother say quietly, "See, I told you we had to let him figure some things out for himself."

Sunday night, Anne and Jack were expected for dinner. They'd been trading weekends between Portland, Oregon, where she worked, and Whispering Oaks, where Jack taught at the high school. Anne had finally found her soul mate—especially after Jack had popped the question. Come September he'd join the family. Lucas hadn't seen Anne this happy, well, ever.

After Lucas finished working on the Mustang he took a shower, planning to show up right on time so as not to seem antisocial.

"Dinner's ready!" His mother called out just as he finished getting dressed. He congratulated himself on perfect planning.

Lucas nearly skidded to a halt when he saw Jocelyn sitting at the dining table next to his sister. How was he supposed to face Joss in broad daylight and not react when all he'd thought about since last night was being naked with her?

"Here." Mom handed him a baking dish filled with lasagna. "Take this to the table for me."

"Good evening," Jocelyn said, a teasing tone to her voice.

"And good evening to you, too." That was as flirty as he'd allow, not ready to advertise their new status as lovers. After putting the dish on the table, he sat next to her and across from Anne, who had a suspicious expression on her face, as if adding up two and two.

Could everyone tell?

"Jack, how're you doing? I hear congratulations are in order." Lucas reached across the table to shake Jack's hand to distract himself.

"Yep. Finally got Anne to come to her senses," Jack said.

His parents couldn't have looked happier if they'd won the million-dollar lottery.

Anne blushed, then kissed Jack on the cheek.

Lucas flashed back to their conversation in the garage where she'd asked him if he believed in finding a soul mate, glad she'd found hers.

Normal dinner chitchat—sprinkled with a fair share of wedding talk—ensued, but it took all of Lucas's control to keep his eyes off Jocelyn. She'd worn a cute little black top that had several slits on the sleeves, giving a peekaboo view of her shoulders. And now he knew those shoulders all too well. Damn, she knew what she was doing, and it nearly drove him nuts.

Finally, dinner was over. Lucas had hardly gotten through it when his dad interrupted his thoughts. "Does everyone have time to play a board game with me?" Kieran said. "I've been going stir-crazy being cooped up in the house all the time."

"Sure," Anne said. "I'm all packed and Jack's going to take me to the airport."

From the look on Jack's face, Lucas got the impression Jack may have wanted a little more private time with Anne before he sent her home. Long-distance relationships had to suck. Every chance they got, Anne and Jack looked at each other or touched. She'd talk and lean into him. Jack actually ate his entire dinner single-handed because his other arm was around Anne, stroking her shoulder as if never wanting to let her go.

"I'd like to, too," Jocelyn said, causing Lucas to mirror Jack's not-so-excited expression.

"Let's play that game where you fib about stuff and try to get others to believe you!" His mom went rushing down the hall to the closet where they stored their family games.

"What about the dishes?" Lucas heard himself ask, sounding incredibly lame.

His mother was back in a flash, board game in hand. "Forget about them for now. You can help me wash them later. Right now it's so nice to have the family together."

The family. Hmm. Was she counting Jocelyn as part of their family? Lucas started feeling boxed in, like he needed to get outside for some fresh air. He glanced at Jocelyn, who must have picked up on his discomfort.

"I'll be Lark's substitute tonight," she said.

His dad smiled, obviously thinking about his youngest daughter all the way back in Boston. His favorite, as Anne and Lucas had decided early on.

A half hour into a less-than-exciting game, everyone got sidetracked with cookies and ice cream. Jack and Lucas brought the last of the bowls out. Lucas handed one to his father, and they smiled at each other.

Lucas could tell how much it meant for his dad to have the family around.

"Do me a favor, Lucas," he said. "Bring out that photo album I put on my dresser."

Oh, God, no. He wasn't planning to embarrass and bore everyone with family photos. Lucas hid his initial reaction. "Sure. We gonna see pictures of you with mutton-chop sideburns?"

He heard his father's boisterous laugh as he retrieved the singled-out family album, deciding not to take any sneak-preview peeks.

"Here you go."

With great pride, his dad shared photos of the kids from twenty years ago: Anne skidding down the Slip 'n Slide with Mom looking on and clapping; Lark on the old swing set, feet extended, high in the sky; Dad tossing a pitch to Lucas, earnestly holding the bat, his tongue at the corner of his mouth in concentration; Jocelyn and Lucas skinny-dipping in the backyard blow-up six-inch-deep wading pool.

Very different from the last time he'd seen her naked.

"See here?" his dad said to Jocelyn. "You were always at our house, like our fourth kid."

Jocelyn blushed, taking the photo album to see how

many pictures she was in. Lucas smiled, remembering how she was always hanging around their house.

The old photos sparked a handful of memories for everyone, and they also made Mom's eyes shine with moisture.

"Lucas, do you remember the time you got me in trouble for laughing in Sunday school?" Anne said, spooning ice cream into her mouth.

"He did that to you, too?" Jocelyn said, licking the back of her ice cream spoon without a clue how much that turned him on.

How had he gotten so many people in trouble in Sunday school? He pulled in his chin. "Who, me?"

"You used to pretend to lisp when we sang hymns." Anne giggled with the memory.

Lucas laughed along with everyone else, catching his mother's adoring eye. He lifted his shoulders. "What can I say? I had a knack."

After everyone finished dessert, Jack and Anne had to leave. He noticed Jocelyn hanging around the door with them. She'd worn straight-leg jeans and boots with a whole bunch of buckles on the sides. Combined with that top, she looked sexy as hell. *Walk her home, idiot.*

"Joss, wait up, I'll walk you home."

After everyone said their goodbyes, Lucas and Jocelyn strolled up her steps. Memories of everything that had happened last night flooded his head. He needed to take a step back and process what it meant to have crazy sex with a lifelong family friend who just happened to be the girl next door.

"You want to come in?" Jocelyn said, a mischievous twinkle in her eyes. Or maybe it was just the porch light.

"I better not. We could get in trouble in there."

"That's kind of what I was hoping."

He lifted a clump of her hair and placed it behind her shoulder. "I don't want my parents to know everything that goes on in my life. Maybe we need to be more discreet, you know?"

She tilted her chin up and because he couldn't resist, he brushed his lips over hers. He wanted to plant hot kisses all over her body, watch her writhe with pleasure the way she had last night—but not tonight. Not when Mom and Dad were next door waiting for him. He couldn't let things get out of hand until he figured out what having sex with Jocelyn meant.

She playfully pushed his chest away. "Okay, then. Not tonight, honey. I have a headache." Her challenging grin did the trick.

He grabbed her wrist, tugged her close and covered her mouth. He breathed in her marshmallow scent with their open and heavy kisses, wanting to eat her up, pushing her against the front door, leaning into her. Her hands were as busy as his, finding his buns and squeezing, pulling him closer and closer.

So much for discreet—standing under the porch light right next door and across the street from snoopy Mr. Cota. In a tricky and impressive move, she turned the door handle from behind and had them inside in the next second.

It was dark. She didn't turn on the lights.

They never made it past the foyer.

An hour later he quietly opened his front door, hoping to sneak inside and go directly to his room. What was it about Jocelyn that made his common sense fly out the window? Until he figured that out, he'd have to steer clear because being in close proximity to Jocelyn led him not only into her arms but into her bed.

Two days later when Lucas hadn't so much as called, Jocelyn combed her hair while getting dressed for school and tried not to freak out. Had she come on too strong and scared him away? The last thing she wanted was for Lucas to think she was stalking him. Multitasking, she decided to leave her hair down for school and to wait for Lucas to make the next move.

Deep inside, she remembered always being the one to seek out Lucas. This time, she'd like things to be different. They'd had fantastic sex, several ways. So why the heck hadn't he knocked on her door since Sunday night?

Driving to school, she couldn't keep him out of her mind. He'd been everything she'd ever wanted in a lover. There was no awkwardness, no game playing, no phony or obligated words, just two old friends finally getting it on. Somehow she'd always known it would be that way.

Not that she'd been planning this her whole life or anything.

She parked in her assigned spot at school, grateful she had a full day. Heck, she had a super-busy week, what with the annual STAR testing for all grades and the final track meet on Saturday. She'd take advantage of being swamped and try to forget Lucas hadn't called. Yet.

"Ack!" she grumbled as she walked into the school, determined not to be the one to make first contact since sex. It would be a long week if she had to wait until Saturday to see him again.

The next Saturday morning, Lucas sat watching his dad. He was off the hook from helping Jocelyn with track meets after the success of the fund-raiser when several more teachers stepped forward since pay was involved, but he couldn't miss today. Besides, he hadn't seen his father so excited since the W.O. track team had taken the regionals and sent three runners on to the state finals in 2002. His dad used a cane to help balance his still-weak leg, but the smile on his face, shadowed by his coach's cap, stretched from earlobe to earlobe.

Lucas had thought about Jocelyn every day, but he couldn't let himself get pulled into her charm again. Until he had something to offer her, there was just no point in moving forward. She was like a drug to him, and he couldn't let himself get addicted. Not yet, anyway.

In the meantime, he'd kept himself distracted with putting the finishing touches on the Mustang and attending a live virtual-college fair. There, he discovered a possible degree in sports and health sciences—that is, if he could swing it on his GI Bill budget. But he had options, for a change. Athletic training had piqued his interest, and he'd also done research on becoming a physician's assistant, which paid well and would utilize a lot of his medic training. But he hadn't made any solid decisions yet. As it was, he'd have to get a job and save as much as possible while taking all the needed basic ed courses. He didn't like the idea of being an almost-thirty-year-old student amid all the local and recent high school grads. Could he be humble enough to handle it?

After settling in the stands, his mom dabbed sunscreen on his dad's nose, then covered her face and neck before donning a sun visor with the school logo on it. Lucas reminded himself there would be gunfire at the beginning of the races and decided to sit on the end of the bleachers in case he needed to make a quick getaway.

He spotted Jocelyn on the field, probably giving last-minute directions to all of her new assistant coaches and the visiting team. Her limp was barely noticeable, but the bandage was still in place. She looked damn cute under her ball cap, whistle hanging around her neck, clipboard in hand, ponytail flapping and school windbreaker billowing in the breeze. Seeing her for the first time since last weekend, when they'd screwed each other's brains out, sent a quick hot jolt through his center. He'd tried his best to forget about her all week, but each night when he crashed, his mind gravitated to Joss and how great she'd felt tucked in his arms. He'd missed her.

Lucas's hands clinched tightly on his knees when the starter fired the first shot for the sprints. Just as quickly, there was a second shot. False start. It seemed the runners were as jumpy as he was. His pulse stuttered in his chest. But he hung on. By the time the middle- and long-distance races rolled around, he'd gotten to where he only flinched and had short-lived palpitations with the shots.

Surrounded by adoring former students, his dad ran an ongoing commentary, which distracted Lucas at first but wore on him after a while. He'd tuned out his father by the 800-meter run. To his mother's credit, she remained engrossed in every word of wisdom coming from her husband's mouth, right along with three former students and their parents. When they started the mile race, Lucas noticed Jocelyn was over with the shot put and discus throwers, and he decided to wander over and say hello.

She glanced up, and a sweet pink blush spread across her cheeks. They hadn't seen each other since last Sunday night, rolling around in the dark on the tile floor of her house, and his body started reacting twenty yards away. He'd avoided her on purpose, but nothing should have stopped her, and she hadn't exactly come looking for him, either. He'd thought about her, though. Oh, yeah, he'd thought about her a lot—and in some very interesting positions.

"What's up?" he said.

"Hey." She could play nonchalant just as well as he could. "Can you believe how great we're doing?"

"I never had a doubt." He squeezed her arm but stopped himself from kissing her cheek.

"Even our discus guys are kicking butt today. It's like a miracle."

"I don't think it's as much a miracle as your hard work paying off."

She glanced at him as if afraid to admit she had anything to do with today's results. "I was lucky to inherit a bunch of talented athletes, is what it is."

"I saw those so-called 'talented' athletes a few practices ago, remember? They were totally undisciplined and taking advantage of you."

"They weren't that bad."

"Half of them didn't even show up for practice on time. You got wise and took control, made them accountable to you and the rest of the team. It's you. Your hard work is paying off today."

She started to blush again, even kicked the dirt with her sneaker, still unwilling to shout to the world that she was far more than a cheerleader.

All coaches on the field.

The request came over the speaker system as Jocelyn lifted her brows. "I gotta go. See you later?"

"I'll be around." After she left, he bought three hot dogs and sodas from the booster-club stand, with the excuse of supporting the school and track team, and headed back to the bleachers to share them with his parents.

His dad couldn't contain himself. "Jocelyn's a natural. Look at how she's got this whole meet under control. Everything's working like clockwork. I'm really impressed."

"Yeah," Lucas said. "She's something else."

So much for having it under control. When the gun went off for the first of the girls' hurdles, Lucas choked on a bite of hot dog. His mom patted his back as if he was still ten years old. He pulled his ball cap closer to his brows after he recovered.

Race after race, the competition was stiff, with several photo finishes, a few contentions and a handful of disappointed runners along with the winners. Once, Lucas caught a sad and distant look in his father's eyes, as if he'd realized, ready or not, it was time to pass on the mantle of head coach.

Lucas sat in the Whispering Oaks sunshine, its warmth massaging his neck and back, a gentle breeze keeping the temperature near perfect. With green farmland off in the distance and a blue-like-baby-eyes sky, Lucas realized how good it felt to be back home, enjoying the morning with his family and watching the girl who'd recently blown his mind take her team to victory.

If anyone had told him this would happen ten years ago, he would have accused them of being crazy.

He watched Jocelyn stride up to a group of track and field officials in a heated discussion over the latest tight finish in the 4-by-100-meter relay. Showing all the confidence in the world, she seemed to hold her own in resolving the debate.

Today, the only person who seemed to be crazy was Lucas for thinking about attending an online university in a field of study he'd never once in his life considered before, just so he had something to offer.

He was crazy about something else, too. Crazy about Joss.

Chapter Ten

Lucas put the finishing touches on the Mustang, washing and waxing it, adjusting the rearview mirror, letting the car idle. The new paint job sparkled in the afternoon sun, classic-car-show ready.

Try as he might he couldn't get Jocelyn out of his mind.

"Are you hungry?" his mother called out the back door. "I've got food on the table, since we forgot lunch."

He glanced at his watch. It was already five o'clock, and he hadn't eaten since that hot dog at the track meet. In his mother's world a hot dog was considered a snack. Turning off the engine, he dusted off his jeans and washed his hands at the patio sink, then went inside. A little burst of adrenaline in his center caught him off guard when he saw Jocelyn already sitting at the table with his dad. Again. Had she become an honorary member of the family or something?

Streams of afternoon sun made her sparkle prettier than his car. She wore a bright pink floral-patterned sundress with a short white sweater, and her hair was down. He especially liked it that way. Parting naturally down the middle, the beckoning cinnamon highlights made him want to dig his fingers in it and kiss her.

"Hi! I hope you don't mind me homing in again, but your mom invited me."

"We're celebrating her win today," Kieran said, already sitting at the head of the table.

"I'm glad you're here," Lucas said, taking a seat across from Jocelyn so he could keep looking at her but not be tempted to grab her in front of his parents.

"You know me. I'd just as soon cook for ten instead of two or three." Beverly brought a large bowl of fresh fruit salad to the table. "Dig in, everyone."

She'd roasted a chicken and made potato salad and her signature skinny coleslaw. It was only mid-May, but the meal seemed more like a summer picnic. Lucas wasn't complaining as he accepted the basket of crusty sourdough rolls thrust at him by his mother.

With the glimmer in Jocelyn's milk-chocolate eyes, and the constant smile stretched across her face, she looked like a lady dying to tell a secret. He would've loved to be the first to know what it was, have her whisper it in his ear. Take it from there. Taking a bite out of a chicken leg, he passed a subversive gaze at her and enjoyed watching her squirm as her cheeks pinked to the same color as her dress. Whatever the secret was she was keeping, it looked as though she'd burst soon if she didn't let it out.

Jocelyn let Kieran replay all the great moments of the track meet for her, like the finish-line lunge controversy by the Rio Mesa sprinter.

"We call that breasting the tape," his dad said, as if Lucas had never been on a track team in his life. "It's one thing to lean into the finish, but some guys throw themselves ahead. That isn't always considered fair. Good call today, though, Jocelyn."

Beverly chimed in with what a great job she'd done talking the Whispering Oaks runner into accepting the outcome. Even Lucas paid her a compliment for whipping the team into shape in time for the finals. The team had won by overall points, and all their strongest runners had set new personal-best times. It had been a good day.

After helping clear the table, Jocelyn suggested Beverly let Lucas and her do the dishes. When his mother didn't immediately agree, Jocelyn insisted she take her coffee and sit out back with Kieran and enjoy the warm late afternoon. The minute she was out of earshot, Jocelyn turned to Lucas.

"I wanted you to be the first to know that I've decided to take you up on your suggestion."

"You mean that kinky little position I mentioned the other night?"

She hit him with a damp dish towel. "About applying for the head coach job. Though maybe we can discuss that other topic later?" For someone focused on a mission, she still managed to cast him a smoldering glance, his immediate reaction landing somewhere below the belt.

He winked and handed her a washed bowl, liking how she made him feel all warm and edgy. She dutifully dried it, but even her drying skills turned him on. Since when had washing dishes become sexy?

"I want to talk to your dad first, so don't say anything, okay?"

"My lips are sealed—see?" He moved them close so she could inspect them, then kissed her quickly before handing her a large fruit-patterned platter to dry.

When they finished the dishes, she set two glasses filled with iced tea on the counter, sliding her hands over her skirt, preparing to carry them outside. "Wish me luck."

He held her by the shoulders and kissed her soundly on the mouth, taking his time to make sure she knew exactly how much luck he wished her. When he'd finished, he enjoyed the dazed look in her eyes. "Good luck."

"Mom!" he called out, throwing Jocelyn out of the sexy haze and causing her to screw up her face from the sudden blast. "Come and show me where all these dishes go, please."

Jocelyn passed Beverly while heading out the door. The woman cast her a knowing glance, even patted her shoulder. It had always been hard to keep secrets from the Gradys.

"I brought you some tea, Coach," she said as she sat beside Kieran, whose healing leg was propped on another chair. Bart sat attentively at Kieran's side, demanding his owner pet his head and scratch underneath his ears.

"Thanks, Jocelyn. Hey, before you say anything, I want you to know that I've had a lot of time to think these past several weeks, and I've made some decisions." He gave a direct look, his crystal-blue eyes more noticeable than usual. "I've come to realize running the entire track program is one hell of a big responsibility, one I'm not so sure I want to carry all by myself anymore."

"After pinch-hitting for you this season, I know exactly what you mean. So, would you mind my asking what your plans are?"

Kieran took a long drink of tea and stared at his outstretched leg and foot on the adjacent chair. He let go a long sigh. "I've decided to step down as head coach." He glanced up to catch her reaction. She was positive he'd seen her eyebrows shoot up and her lips part, even though she'd shut her mouth the instant it had dropped open. "I'm thinking I'd be better suited to be in a more supportive role from now on, let someone else carry the full load."

"Really? You're surprising me, Coach."

He patted her knee. "Oh, hell, Jocelyn, you've already proved yourself. I think you should get the extra pay, too, and nothing could make me happier if you're the one to replace me."

She tucked some hair behind one ear. "I *have* been giving it some serious thought, but only because I sort of wondered if you were thinking about giving up the job. Lucas hinted that you were."

"After the accident, I had to do a lot of thinking. Look, if I could handpick someone, it would be you." He took his ball cap off his head, scratched his forehead and replaced the cap. "Do you want the job?"

"I do. I really do."

"Then fill out the paperwork because as far as I'm concerned, it's yours. But I'm warning you that that jack-off Schuster might want to try for it, too. Beat him to it!"

She jumped up, threw her arms around his neck and squeezed. "I won't let you down, Coach. I promise."

He smiled at her, all his craggy lines deepening. "I have no doubt about that, Coach."

Jocelyn found Lucas in his favorite place, the garage, tinkering with the Mustang. She ran up and threw her arms around his back, hugging him tight.

"So what's the word?" He turned so he could return the embrace.

"The word is I'm applying for the head coach job first thing Monday morning."

He lifted and swung her around while they continued to hug. "Fantastic."

"I know, huh?" When he put her down, she kissed

him the way she'd wanted to earlier in the kitchen, when he practically made her knees knock with his taunting kiss. His arms and hands found all the right places on her body to make her feel welcomed. She'd gotten used to his skills way too fast. Somehow, with Lucas, innocent kisses always turned quickly into smokin' hot invitations to rip each other's clothes off. But it being broad daylight, and them being within view of the back porch where she presumed the Gradys sat, she fought for control.

Lucas must have been on the same wavelength because he ended the kiss before she was ready. She liked the burning look he gave and wanted to turn it into a flash fire at the first opportunity.

"I forgot to tell you how sexy you look today," he said.

"Thanks." As if she'd never heard a compliment before, and especially under his thorough head-to-toe inspection, she felt her cheeks warm.

"You know, you're not the only one with news."

She leaned her elbows on the hood of the car. "What? Tell me, tell me."

"I've been looking into sports medicine programs online and found some options I might be interested in. And I've signed up for a couple of online basic ed courses at Marshfield C.C."

Thrilled by the news, she stood at attention. "This is great!"

"I've been thinking," he said, leaning against the car, arms folded nonchalantly. "A special day like today needs an extra special way to celebrate." He opened the passenger side of the Mustang. "What do you say we take this baby for its first spin around town?"

She clapped her hands like a kid. "That's a perfect idea."

"Hop in, Coach."

She bussed his cheek as she slid inside the 1965 Mustang and onto the newly reupholstered white leather seats.

When he got in the car, he returned a light kiss on her lips, then turned on the definitely updated radio, which happened to be playing a Black Eyed Peas song, "I Gotta Feeling." In her mind, it already *was* a good night. A great night.

An hour later, after driving around with the top down, listening to upbeat music and stopping for ice cream, they headed out of town. They drove past prime farmland, smelling pungent onions and sweetening strawberries, through walnut and orange groves with their citrusy scent and up a winding road in the Serena Vista hills to a panoramic view of the Whispering Oaks valley. Though her hair was knotted and messy from the wind, she didn't care—she was with Lucas. Everything was good and today had already been one of the best in her entire life.

He parked, and they both hopped out of the car to take in the impressive view.

"I forgot how beautiful it is up here," he said, gazing across the entire valley.

"Remember when we had our prom in that airplane hangar over there?" She pointed to another hill-top across the way, with obvious signs of some sort of party going on right then.

He gave a sullen nod, having hated his prom. The only thing on his mind that night had been getting inside his date's pants. Then he'd left town for boot camp right after he graduated and never looked back. Not very noble, but that was who he was back then.

She took his hand in hers. "I held out to the last minute before accepting my date, hoping you might ask me."

He laughed and shrugged, though he felt both touched and melancholy at once. Hindsight was sometimes a bitch. "Believe me, you would have had a terrible time with me. I only went because Mom and Dad made me. Gave me the old line about 'this will only happen once in your life.'" He drew her into his arms and rested his chin on her head. "I remember seeing a picture of you afterward, and you looked pretty." He kissed the top of her smooth hair. "Very pretty in pink. Just like today. Did I tell you I like that dress?"

She hugged a bit tighter and glanced up at him. "Yes, you did. Thank you."

He kissed her before she could finish thanking him, and warmth bled through him, forcing ideas about permanence and giving his new life a fair chance. Maybe Jocelyn could help him get things straight again.

As always, whenever they kissed, his body reacted, craving more. He held her hips close to his growing response and let her kiss him deeper and longer. Hell, these days, with her fingers roaming over his scalp, he even had hair to mess up. The thought made him smile.

"What," she said across his lips.

"What do you mean, 'what'? I'm kissing you."

"You're smiling. I can feel it." She kissed around his lips; he chased her kisses. "Admit it," she said.

He pulled back and looked into her eyes, enjoying her coy game. "That I'm hot for you? That's an understatement."

She lightly slapped his chest, a self-satisfied gaze in her beckoning eyes. "That you like being home."

He took her cue and dug his fingers into her hair, kissed her like he was leaving town first thing tomorrow morning, then pulled back to watch her recover. Damn, that dewy-eyed look never got old. He loved how she always answered his touch, egged him on for more. The ever-tightening package in his jeans reminded him how he never failed to react to her, too. "I like being with you. I know that much."

She sighed, as if he'd said the most perfect answer in the universe, and they held each other and enjoyed the view, watching the setting sun shift the sky into the color of peaches, then bright orange just before turning deep red.

A vibrating boom, quickly followed by scattershot sounds, cut to his core. He jerked and held Jocelyn tighter, scanning the horizon for the source of fire. Except her gasp was one of joy, and she felt like butter in his arms.

"Look," she said. "Fireworks. It's from the party

going on over there. Maybe it's a birthday or a wedding or something." She pointed to the airplane hangar again, where there were more explosions followed by bursts of color, splattering and dripping down the evening sky.

Lucas took a deep breath, glad he hadn't freaked out at the sudden noise and the blasts of ongoing fireworks. The sound was too close to gunfire, reminding him of far too many encounters over in the sandbox. Sounds that ensured injury and loss of life. He needed to relax. Focus on Jocelyn.

She rubbed his back and dropped her head on his shoulder as they stood and watched the entire show. He willed her mood to rub off on him, to take away the peripheral images threatening to become center stage in his mind.

"I talked to my parents today," she said. "Told them all about the track meet."

"How are they?"

"Great. They've decided to stay on the road in their RV another few months, so looks like I'll be your next-door neighbor awhile longer, just me and the dogs."

"I like that plan." Though he didn't honestly know where he'd be in the near future. He hadn't made up his mind yet.

"You can stay over whenever you want."

"Whoa, whoa, we're just getting to know each other."

She stepped in front of him and took his face in her hands. "Lucas Grady, I've known you my whole life."

"You've got a point there." After an initial tensing,

he got to thinking how much more privacy he could have at Jocelyn's house than in his old bedroom under his parents' constant scrutiny. He'd be right next door if they needed his help. But what would Mom and Dad think about his shacking up with the girl next door?

Jocelyn seemed suddenly quiet. Wisely, she'd let the subject drop. How could he commit to frequent flyer status with her when he hadn't yet made up his mind about what he wanted to do with the rest of his life?

She turned back around and he snuggled with her in his arms because that felt so much better than thinking about the future or the plans he'd yet to nail down. After a while, he let down his guard and enjoyed the near-fourth-of-July display. With his mind focused on the big show, and with her body pressing close to his, another kind of fireworks twined through his thoughts—the kind he made with Jocelyn.

"What do you say I take you home?" he asked when the flashy display finished.

"Will you stay with me?" she whispered.

"I'll do anything you want as long as we're naked."

In the middle of the night, with Jocelyn tightly spooned against Lucas's back, a subdued growl coaxed her out of deep sleep. His body stiffened and jerked. She held on, trying to soothe him away from his fitful dream. He settled for a few seconds, then tensed again, legs kicking, arms flailing, a muffled yell starting from what seemed like the soles of his feet worked its way up to his tightly closed mouth. His arms flew up, his elbow catching Jocelyn in the face as he bolted out of the bed, still completely out of it.

Shocked by the hit to her cheek, she rolled off the bed, turned on the light and stayed out of his way. His lids flew open. Sweat glistened on his chest, fear and panic plagued his unseeing eyes. Torment etched his face. His breathing was a ragged mess. So was hers as she stood pressed against the wall in the corner, waiting for him to quit fighting ghosts and wake up.

She wanted to hold him, to somehow comfort him, but it was too dangerous. The coppery taste of blood proved she needed to stay out of his path. Wait for him to come around.

The lighted bed lamp must have filtered through to his brain because he came back to consciousness, his wide-open, terrorized eyes finally seeing. He stood completely still, the only movement being his eyes darting back and forth, as if clicking back into reality one breath at a time, slowly comprehending what he'd done.

She couldn't help it—she trembled and licked the corner of her mouth, where fresh blood continued to gather. He looked so damn distressed. Tears filled her eyes as she finally saw firsthand the anguish Lucas dealt with. She'd had no idea. How could she?

"Joss? Oh, my God, I'm sorry." He rushed around the bed. "I'm so sorry."

Overcome with the sudden outburst she'd witnessed, her knee-jerk reaction was to bolt, but he was awake now—she could stop shuddering.

"Joss, baby." He reached for her. She recoiled involuntarily but caught herself and took his hand.

"Please. I'm awake. I'm okay, now. God, I'm so sorry."

She chanced another look into his eyes. He was completely alert. Remorse etched deeply across his twisted features.

"Baby—" He stepped beside her. "Forgive me. I'm so sorry."

Hating feeling scared, she let him touch her. "It's okay," her voice quivered. "You must've had a honking-bad nightmare."

He enfolded her in his arms, and she leaned into him, realizing he still trembled and needed something to hold on to as much as she did. "Maybe all the gunfire at the track meet and the fireworks tonight got to you."

"Maybe. Who knows." He brought her back to the bed and left her there while he walked to the bathroom, ran some water and returned with a cold washcloth to dab at her lip.

"Now do you see?" he said. "I'm no good for you."

More tears brimmed and washed over her lids. "You've been through a lot, Lucas." If only she could get her voice to sound normal. "You can get help." She let him doctor her lip, then took hold of his hands again, an attempt to let him know she wasn't scared anymore.

Or was it an attempt to convince herself?

Once he was satisfied her mouth had stopped bleeding, he gently kissed her lips. "You're the only help I need right now."

Then, slowly and meticulously, he made love to her. Beginning with her neck and breasts, he touched and sampled every inch of her skin, helping them both forget the nightmare he'd lived and she'd just witnessed.

As his damp stomach pressed into hers with each slow and thorough thrust, she completely gave in, realizing how precious sex was with him. With her hips answering each of his lunges, she did her best to show him she loved him, and as her reward shuddered through her, she could have sworn she'd heard him say, "I never want us to end."

Chapter Eleven

Lucas rushed through the front door Sunday morning, only to find his mother wearing her big yellow bathrobe and standing with a cup of coffee in her hand, open-eyed and observing his every move.

"Hey," he said and continued to walk down the hall. Anything to get away from her scrutiny.

With his mother being as intuitive as she'd always been, there was no way she'd miss that something was seriously wrong. And she'd basically caught him on a walk of shame, to boot. Yet she had the good sense to keep her mouth shut about it. "And good morning to you, too," she answered after taking a sip.

He strode to his room, closing the door harder than he'd intended. After turning on his computer he fired off an email to one of his army buddies, Jake, back in North Carolina. They were two peas in a pod: made it through a couple of tours in Afghanistan together, lost a friend to an IED, suffered from PTSD. Jake had left Lucas with an open invitation just before he came home, and it was time to take him up on it.

Is that offer to be roommates still on?

If he was serious about becoming an athletic trainer, he could do it anywhere because many of the classes could be taken online with a mentor. Ditto for PA school, and that would only take three years because he was medic trained. As soon as he'd gotten a degree and these PTSD issues settled down, once he had *something to offer* Jocelyn, then he'd consider being her roommate and a hell of a lot more.

If she'd wait for him.

Regardless, until then he'd bite the bullet and break the news to her, then take the heat. Or, he could forget the whole thing, reenlist, go back to the desert, stay out of people's hair. But they were drawing down the troops, now.

He was damaged goods. The last thing Jocelyn deserved was another wing nut like her ex-fiancé interfering with her life, and Lucas wasn't going to do that to her. Period.

It wasn't like he was walking away forever—he was just postponing Jocelyn's "let's be roommates" plan.

The big question was—would she understand his reasoning? Not likely.

When she called Sunday evening, he made an excuse that he was exhausted and needed to get some sleep, then cut the conversation short. He couldn't bear the thought of seeing her swollen lip and knowing he'd given it to her. On Monday afternoon, he left a message at her house before she got home from school that he was taking a ride into L.A. on business. He wasn't lying, either. He'd contacted his old high school buddy from auto shop, David, and discovered he had his own auto body business in the valley.

Because Lucas's mind was whirling in a thousand different directions, he discussed an apprenticeship to take his love of renovating cars one step further. Then Lucas spent the rest of the week hanging out and learning new techniques in auto body repair.

They were all options. Nothing was set in stone. If he was serious about being a man Jocelyn could love and respect, he needed plans. He needed time and space to process what direction he'd take his life. He couldn't very well be a soldier in a civilian world. Hell, he was twenty-eight. It was time to figure things out.

His mother's inquisitive eyes grew more intense as the week progressed, and he'd obviously been dodging Jocelyn. *Are you afraid of intimacy?* she seemed to convey with her watchful glances.

Who, me?

Friday evening, after tearing his brain apart all week weighing the choices, Lucas decided to man up and face Jocelyn to tell her exactly where he stood. He took a shower and shaved, even dabbed on some new aftershave. He threw on some jeans and a long-sleeved T-shirt his mother had bought him with some designer's name stamped along the bottom. He at least wanted to look nice for Jocelyn when he broke the news he'd finally figured out.

Jocelyn had run out of patience with Lucas. This incommunicado business stunk to high heaven. She sat at the kitchen table wearing baggy sweats, nibbling at a totally unappealing salad and staring out the window at the rolling brown hills. He'd avoided her all week, after they'd reached a new level of closeness, and it hurt like a knife in the liver.

If she hadn't had school midterms to deal with, she would have been in his face by Wednesday. But she had a job to do, and she didn't take her teaching career lightly, so she sucked up all her worries and fears about Lucas pulling back from her and forced herself to get through the week. Once the weekend came, she'd confront him and force him to talk to her.

But in the meantime, she couldn't avoid wondering what in the world was going on in Lucas's mind. Sure, he'd scared her, and she'd been shaken up, but she knew the difference between being bullied and being an innocent bystander to an ex-soldier's nightmare. He had PTSD. In her heart, she knew he'd never hurt her.

He'd promised he'd never hurt her that night. Over and over he'd begged her forgiveness before he made love to her so thoroughly that she'd have to be crazy not to forgive and forget. He'd touched her everywhere as if she were a delicate flower, driving her crazy with desire for him, and then he devoured her with his passion, sweeping her away to places she'd only ever been with him. No one could be that tender one moment and out of control with desire the next without feeling something special right down to the core. Obviously, he was only promising to never hurt her physically, not cause physical pain, but the emotional kind of pain, the kind that ate deeper through her heart each day he stayed away, felt much harder to bear.

Her stomach cramped, but she forced herself to eat.

She was tough and adaptable; she could handle their situation. If he'd just give her a fair chance.

She took a tasteless bite of salad leaves. The question of all questions being—did Lucas believe himself? Did he really think he could harm her? More important, could he believe *in* himself the way she believed in him? That was something only he could do for himself.

She heard a tapping at her front door. After rinsing her food down with water, she folded her napkin, flipped it on the table and marched to answer it, quelling her quickening heartbeat on the way.

She opened the door and found Lucas looking like a god—clean and dressed to kill in tight jeans and a form-fitting black knit shirt. Her pulse zigzagged in her chest. Why hadn't she changed out of the gray sweats? His broad shoulders and narrow hips never ceased to amaze her. But she was mad at him, damn it, and she couldn't let him off the hook just for looking hunky. "Hi, stranger."

"Hey. Can I come in?"

Without another word, she opened the door so he could pass. Both Daisy and Diesel had come to meet him, and they licked his hands. He bent down to greet each of them face to face, looking so damn cute and making sure his sexy behind was on display. Nope. She was not going to fall for his "I'm good with animals, how can you resist me" bit, either.

She didn't offer him a seat, but he went to the couch anyway. Though her hospitality instincts pushed to click in by asking if he wanted a drink, she kept her mouth shut. Instead, she took a long, quiet breath.

He sat, legs wide, an ankle resting on the opposite knee, trying to look comfortable but far from it. He'd pushed his sleeves up his forearms and the muscles distracted her...briefly.

"So you're probably wondering where I've been all week."

She plopped down on the far end of the couch and wished she had put on makeup after her shower. "You got that right."

His lips made a straight line and he nodded.

Damn it, she could smell his tangy scent all the way across the couch, and he'd obviously just gotten out of the shower because his hair was damp and combed sexily back. She wanted to take her sweatshirt hood and cover her head.

She swallowed the plethora of angry questions she had and the perturbed thoughts she'd accumulated with each passing day of the week. She stuffed back down the nagging, insecure thoughts that threatened to rip her wide open. *What's wrong with me? Why can't you love me?* Lack of communication could drive a girl to unconfident conclusions. Old habits and lagging self-worth had muddled her thoughts.

He cleared his throat. "So, I've been doing a lot of thinking this week, and I've decided to go back to school."

Fantastic, but dare she let herself get excited yet? He was going back to school—and she'd encouraged him to do it. He'd taken her advice. Yay. He'd be around, and even if he didn't stay involved with her, at least he'd be nearby, hopefully in Whispering Oaks.

Slow down. Slow down.

"That's great." She didn't let her excitement show but kept her voice steady and calm, the exact opposite of her swirling mind and the pulse that was back to trotting in circles in her chest.

"When I go back to school, I'll have to give it my total concentration."

Her heart stumbled. Here comes the "it's not you, it's me" speech. She took a deep breath, waiting for the sucker punch, hoping beyond hope she was wrong about him wanting nothing more to do with her.

His hazel gaze connected with her suspicious stare, and to his credit, he didn't look away. "I'll need a bachelor of science and health degree if I go the route I'm thinking. You know how much effort that will take."

She gave him a single nod as tension seeped over her shoulders and up her neck.

"I've got a buddy in Raleigh who owns a house, and,

well—" he picked at some dog fur on his jeans "—they've got an accredited sports medicine and athletic trainer program—"

She'd heard all she could take. Her breathing had derailed with the mention of Raleigh. Now her fingers trembled; she was so enraged by what he was leading up to. "You made that decision this week?"

He'd been concentrating on the dog fur rather than looking at her. Now his eyes jerked toward her as if he'd realized she had no intention of making this easy on him. "Yes. After giving it a lot of thought."

Obviously, he hadn't been giving her much thought at all. She leaned forward and tapped his knee. "We finally get together and now you plan to leave, and as an afterthought you mention it to me? Did you think maybe we could discuss this since we've been friends all our lives and now we're lovers? Or was I imagining all that?"

"You've got this all wrong. I've been doing nothing but thinking about you."

"So you just go ahead and make your little exit plan without discussing it with me."

"I'm trying to make something out of myself for *you* by going back to school. You said it yourself—I should look into sports medicine. Well, now I have, and I'm interested in sports training, which requires at least a bachelor's degree. I've got my work cut out for me and I'll have to give it total concentration."

"What happened the other night? And the week before that? Did I miss the small print about our having sex? Am I only good enough for a couple of nights, some good times?"

He stopped her finger tapping on his knee, which had gotten more intense along with the conversation, by grabbing her hand. "Joss, you're not a casual date to me. Don't ever think of yourself that way."

"What am I supposed to think?" She yanked her fingers back. "Are all of your casual affairs as intense as what you and I have? Because I've got to tell you, I could have sworn we had something special." Burning had started behind her eyes and, damn it, she knew tears would soon follow. She looked away, biting her lip.

With one hand he gathered both of hers, and with the other, he eased her face back to look at his. "We do have something special." Earnest hazel eyes stared into hers, eyes she wanted with all of her heart to believe. "That's why it's so important to me to find out who I am and what I want to do before I get completely involved with you."

She yanked her chin from his grasp. "I'm so special you've got to run away from me—is that it?" She hated to sound bitter, especially with her chin trembling.

"No. That's not what I'm saying." She could feel his frustration when he dropped her hands and stood up. "Look, I'm going back to school to please you. I want to be something for you. I thought you'd be happy."

Was he trying to make her feel guilty? She wouldn't fall for it.

"I should be happy about losing you? I've only just found you. What are you doing?"

He'd shut down before her eyes. He might have had plans, but that didn't justify his method of dropping a bomb on her. There was no other way to look at it. Did he really think she'd be happy about his leaving the state to go back to school?

She stood to meet his gaze. "What's wrong with the university system right here?" *What's wrong with me?* "Surely there are all kinds of sports medicine programs in California. Do you even give a damn about me?"

He regarded her with hurt in his eyes. "You know I give a damn, Joss, but you've got to let me do this my way. I'm thinking about my future. Our future. I can't offer you a future unless I have one of my own." He paced toward the door.

"I'm willing to go through this with you." She wanted to go after him but forced her feet to stand firm. "We can work this out. Together."

When he reached for the knob, his shoulders stiffened into military attention. "This is what I've decided to do." He looked at the floor, at the dogs reacting to their tense conversation, rather than into her eyes. "You don't need me around freaking you out with my nightmares and mood swings. It's best this way."

"Quit making excuses!" Her hands fisted as she watched him head to the door. "You've always been fine with me just the way you are."

"That's not good enough." Without another word, he let himself out.

Red-hot anger blinded her, and she felt a frustration

so intense it seemed to strangle her. She picked up a pillow from the couch and threw it just as the door shut.

She had to let him do it his way. Did she have a choice? Had he given her one iota of say in the decision?

Her encouraging him had paid off on the going-back-to-school suggestion, but all the cheerleading in the world couldn't change the fact he wasn't sticking around.

Truth was she couldn't coerce Lucas into loving her or staying in Whispering Oaks no matter how much she loved him. Until he was ready to step up, the fact that she'd loved him since she was twelve didn't matter.

Defeat overcame her, and she crumpled onto the couch and cried.

Lucas left Jocelyn's house feeling like the heel of the year. He'd broken his first rule on women—never let anyone get close. When he was in the service, always getting deployed had made it easy to keep that rule. He'd come home and gotten way too close to Jocelyn too quickly. Now he was paying for it. They both were. He saw the hurt in her eyes, as if he'd used her for sex, then cast her aside. It couldn't be further from the truth. He cared about her. He had since they were kids, but this was something more. When he'd made love to her Saturday night after the nightmare, he'd cherished her, every inch of her, made love to her as if she was the only other person on earth. She'd made him feel the same way. No one had ever made him feel like that before.

He didn't know what the hell love felt like because

he'd never gone there. Not once. The aching in his chest as he strode back home, and the gnawing feeling in his throat over hurting her, might be a clue to how falling out of love felt. To use a military term, when things went FUBAR in love.

Entering his house, he whisked by his parents. Both of their heads popped up from watching TV when he passed. He marched straight for his room to grab the keys to the Mustang. Bart followed him halfway down the hall but must have sensed he was unwelcome and turned around.

Rather than face his parents again, Lucas exited through the French doors in their bedroom into the backyard and then the garage. He started the engine and threw the car into drive, even pealed a little rubber when he pulled out of the driveway and onto the street.

White-knuckling the steering wheel, he'd drive until he could breathe again because right now his lungs were tied up in knots and a brick seemed to sit on his diaphragm.

Like a broken record he repeated the same lines to himself. *She deserves someone who knows who they are, where they're going and what they want. Someone who is established and has something to offer her besides jagged nerves and a half-hearted plan to go back to school.*

Once he had a profession, like she did, when he could feel equal to her, he'd have something to bring to the table in their relationship. Right now, being a slacker who loved her wasn't enough.

He loved her? Was he just scared?

How could a guy who'd faced down gunfire and makeshift bombs be a coward? Was letting down all barriers and finally getting close to someone so scary? *Hell, yeah!*

He pushed on the gas, fishtailing around a secluded corner, and drove until the banging pulse in his head and chest let up. When he'd finally calmed down, he headed for home.

Later, on his bed staring at the ceiling in the dark and feeling completely mixed-up and fifteen all over again, his mother tapped on the door.

"Lucas, would you come out for a minute, please?"

This was no time to sit through a lecture from his parents. In fact, it was the last thing he wanted to do, but he was living under their roof and he owed them his consideration. Though for this reason alone, the thought of moving to Raleigh looked better all the time. He rolled off the bed, flipped on the light switch and opened the door. "Yeah, Mom?"

"Jocelyn is here to see you."

Damn. His gut clinched, but he followed his mother down the hall, dreading what he'd find.

The instant he hit the family room, Mom and Dad vanished. Jocelyn, dressed in jeans and a white blouse, stood in the living room by the fireplace. She'd let her hair down from earlier and put on makeup. She looked pretty, as she always did, and he wished he could hold her, but he kept his distance, unsure of what she had to say.

She watched him, a softer gaze in her eyes than earlier.

"Hi," he said.

"Hi." She swallowed. "So after our argument earlier, I decided I needed to apologize to you."

"It's not necessary." Hell, he should be apologizing to her!

"No. It is. I went way over the deep end. I made more out of things than I should have."

"No, you didn't."

That got her attention. She'd been staring at her black flats, but now her eyes darted to his. "I didn't?"

He shook his head.

"So why are you leaving, then?"

He shrugged, feeling like a fool with no good answer. "It's something I've got to do."

"I wish you'd reconsider it, Lucas." She connected with his eyes and wouldn't allow him to look away. Her sweet doe eyes melted the cold corners of his heart, making him want to take back everything he'd said earlier. *I'll do anything you want. Just let me still be with you.* He cleared his throat. *Will you wait for me?* God, he didn't have the right to ask her that.

"I'll see how things go."

She sighed. Her hands covered her face. "Well, if you're hell-bent on leaving, I want you to know something." She looked up with a painful expression, holding his full attention. "I love you. Nothing you do can stop that."

Stunned by her comment, he stood dazed as she reached for the door and let herself out.

He rubbed his face, which seemed to have gone numb. She loved him?

Like an idiot, he hadn't told her he loved her, too.

On Saturday, after a sleepless night, he got up early and spent the day with David, getting more hands-on experience with auto body work. As he concentrated on the task, nothing else entered his mind. It was a welcome relief. He liked the satisfaction of taking twisted and dented metal and making it malleable, easing out the wrinkles until it was smooth and just like new again. It was a slow and meticulous but gratifying process, and he only wished he could apply the technique to himself.

On Sunday morning Lucas walked Bart. "Stop! No," he said as Bart played tug-of-war with the leash to turn onto Jocelyn's yard so Bart could greet his dog friends, Diesel and Daisy. "Sorry, buddy, not today." Lucas yanked back and finally convinced Bart the group walk wasn't going to happen. Halfway over to the grammar school where he intended to let Bart off leash for a romp around the huge fenced-in playground and yard, he got a text message from Jocelyn. She didn't greet him or anything, just sent an address and phone number for a community-based outpatient clinic in Oxnard where they offered group and individual therapy for soldiers.

She wouldn't let up. Once he got past being bugged and letting Bart hear all of his gripes on the walk home, he had to admit he appreciated her caring about him. Especially when he'd essentially dumped her with a lame excuse about moving out of state to go to school.

Just before he reached his house, he texted back—Thanks.

Then he turned off his phone.

It was quiet. *Eight o'clock, the old man must still be sleeping.* He let Bart off leash so he could slurp from his water bowl on the patio, then went to the kitchen to get a drink.

Mom sat at the table in the newly remodeled and extended French country kitchen, head in her hands. Shards of light cut across the table and her bathrobe, tiny dust particles dancing inside. The rich aroma of coffee tempted him to have a cup, but he'd gone off caffeine to see if it would help with his insomnia.

"You okay?" he asked, approaching the table, setting his glass down and putting his hands on his mother's shoulders.

"I'm worried about your sister, is all."

"Last time I checked, she and Jack were just fine."

"I'm talking about Lark. I just got off the phone with her." Mom stared at the cream clouds in her coffee. "She wants to drop out of med school and come home."

"What?" Last he'd checked, Little Miss High Achiever was breezing through her first year of courses at Boston University Medical School. She'd done what Anne had dreamed of but couldn't quite pull off—got into med school. Lark had always wanted to be a pediatrician. Now she wanted to drop out?

"That's what I said. Please don't tell your father. I'm hoping to talk some sense into her."

Lucas downed his water without taking a breath.

"Okay, but it's probably a good idea to give him a heads-up—and soon."

Beverly lifted sad dark brown eyes and studied him. Her face looked more drawn this morning, as if she'd aged a couple years since yesterday. "You haven't been sleeping again, have you?"

He shrugged.

"You're too young to look so tired." She got up and went to the cupboard. "Here. Try this. It's all natural. Three different ingredients to help you sleep. It might help."

"I tried sleeping pills before I came home. Didn't like the way they made me feel all groggy the next day."

"This is a mild homeopathic blend. Why not give it a try? Don't let those dark circles under your eyes ruin your handsome face."

"Okay, Mom." He took the bottle. "I'll try one tonight." After the mess he'd made with Jocelyn, sleep had not come easily, nor did it last very long when it finally did roll around just before dawn each day.

He walked to the coffeemaker, picked up the carafe and refilled her coffee cup. She reached up and patted his hand. "You're a good son. I want to see you happy, Lucas. You deserve to be happy and with someone you love." Her shifted gaze toward the Howards' house didn't go unnoticed. What could he say?

"My Grandma Daniels used to quote some old saying to me. 'From friendship blooms the truest love.' Of course, I scoffed, like I know you're scoffing right now. But when I went away to college I met a lot of guys, dated a few, then when I met your dad there was something different about him. I knew I could be friends with him, first. My granny had been right."

What was he supposed to say to that? Mom had gone in for the kill, knowing he and Jocelyn had a lifetime of friendship behind them. He clenched his jaw, deciding to let his mother have the last word.

"One more thing," she said. "I want you to know how much I've loved having you home and how hard it was for me to let you go away to boot camp when you were only eighteen. I already lost you once ten years ago. Now that I've finally got you back, isn't there some way you can stick around?"

He took a deep breath. "I'm working on it. Honestly."

"A mother never stops worrying about her children, no matter how old they are. Anne has finally found a good man, and now you've got a shot at something real with—"

He lifted his palm to stop her. "Let me deal with this my way. Please?"

His mom lifted her cup and took a sip. "I have no choice. You're a man now. All grown up." She picked up her cell phone as though she wanted to make another call to his little sister.

"You want me to call Lark? Talk to her?"

His mom shook her head. "I'll handle this for now. You've got enough on your plate."

She made an excellent point. His plate was overflowing. If he went away to school, he'd risk losing Jocelyn, but if he stayed here, he wouldn't have a thing to offer her. Either way, he came off looking like a slacker. He took the bottle of homeopathic sleeping pills, thanked his mother and went down the hall to shower.

Monday, he found himself back at the auto body shop, learning every technique he could. Someone brought in the bare bones of another classic Mustang, and Lucas allowed a little dream to take hold about buying more cars and renovating them. Later, David asked him out to lunch, said he had something to discuss with him.

Great. Like he needed more decisions.

Tuesday afternoon, sitting on the hood of his Mustang overlooking the Whispering Oaks valley, he dialed Anne's cell phone.

"Lucas?"

They briefly exchanged the usual niceties. "I wanted to run something by you," he said.

"Sure. Did Mom tell you about Lark?" She'd zoomed right in, but brought in a whole new topic of conversation.

"Yeah. Any idea why she wants to quit school?"

"Lark's not giving me any details, but I'm pretty sure it has to do with a man."

"Of course. Sorry to hear that."

"What do you think is up with all of us?" Anne asked.

"What're you talking about?"

"The three of us—you, me and Lark. We all seem to

run away from the best people. Granted, I don't have a clue what's going on with Lark and whoever, but you... Come on. You and Jocelyn have been a perfect match since you were kids." So she hadn't gone off topic after all.

"Look, I didn't call to talk about my love life, Anne."

"Do you think Mom and Dad screwed us up?"

What the heck was she talking about? "How could they? They have a great marriage."

"I know, but maybe it's so good, none of us think we can live up to it. Maybe we're afraid to fail in front of them."

"Are you saying you're afraid to marry Jack because if you are, I'm here to tell you..."

"No. I'm solid on that. I was thinking about you, Little Brother. I'm suggesting you not do what I tried to do."

Did all the women in his life have to talk in riddles and confuse him? "Is this about that soul-mate business again? Because I'm not buying it."

"Well, maybe you should."

He shrugged at the sky, shook his head and screwed up his face. *Should, what?*

"Buy it."

Damn it, could Anne read minds, too?

With his stomach twisting in a thousand knots, he didn't have the nerve to bring up the real reason he'd called—whether or not to take David up on yesterday's offer. She'd taken him way off path, and he didn't have the strength to bring up the subject of Jocelyn. "Listen, I've got to go."

"Let me ask you the same question you asked me a couple months ago—what do you have back east that you can't find here?"

"That was different, and you know it," he said. Though in his heart he knew it wasn't different at all.

"Quit running, Lucas. Don't do what I did and waste ten years." Okay, she was a mind reader. Eerie. "I gave notice at work today. In another month, I'll be moved out of my apartment in Portland and back home in Whispering Oaks. We could be one big happy family again. I've missed you."

That seemed to be the ongoing theme of all of his conversations lately.

"Maybe I'll stick around until you move home. But I can't promise anything."

"I'd like that. As soon as I find out anything about Lark, I'll let you know."

"You do that. And, Anne?"

"Yes?"

"I'm really happy for you and Jack."

"Thank you, Lucas. So am I. And my fingers are crossed that you'll wake up and admit the best thing in your life is right next door."

"Okay, that's it. I'm outta here." He clicked off before he got ticked off.

The last sound he heard before he hung up was his sister's overconfident laugh. Why did that always bug the hell out of him? Especially when he knew she was right and he was wrong.

Before he could "wake up" like Anne wanted, he needed to have at least one good night's sleep. Mom's hoodoo-voodoo homeopathic pills had helped some, but he still wasn't there yet.

On Thursday, Lucas stayed home to take his dad to the doctor to have his one remaining cast on his arm removed. To give his dad an extra kick on his big day, Lucas drove the Mustang to the appointment.

"You did a fantastic job on this," his dad said, running his hand along the dashboard.

Lucas nodded with pride. "I loved every minute of it, too."

"After today, I'll be almost back to my old self, and you'll be free to make that move you've mentioned."

"Yep."

"It's been great having you around. Do you really have to leave the state?"

Lucas hadn't answered Jake's most recent email asking to finalize the plans. "It's a definite possibility. I like what I saw online about the athletic training program there. There are some excellent physician's assistant programs, too."

"How does Jocelyn feel about your leaving?"

Lucas clenched his jaw. If he ground his molars any harder, they'd push into his gums. "She's not happy about it."

Showing excellent parental restraint, his dad let the subject drop.

* * *

"Mr. Grady, we'll have this cast off in no time."

"Thank the good Lord. I've been through this before with my leg, so let's not waste time explaining anything. Just cut this sucker off my arm, would you?"

The orthopedic technician smiled, then put on protective goggles and revved up the cast cutter. Sounding more like the equipment at the auto body shop than what one would expect at a doctor's office, he sliced through the cast with precision. When it broke free and fell off his arm, Dad sighed with relief and moved his fingers and twisted his wrist to make sure everything still worked.

"Nice scar, Dad."

"Looks like you had a nasty break, Mr. Grady," the technician said.

"I've got the pins and plates to prove it, too. Ah, that's stiff," his dad said as he straightened his elbow. "My arm smells like hell and looks ninety years old, but I gotta tell ya, Lucas, this is the prettiest damn thing I've seen since I first met your mother." He grinned wide. "I'm free! Free at last."

Lucas smiled at his father's excitement. He watched him work out more kinks and thank the technician for his help, then he offered to buy Lucas lunch on the way home.

They pulled into a new sushi restaurant on a ridge with a view of most of the city. It was another clear, cloudless blue-skied day, the usual valley breeze rustling leaves in nearby oaks, and the view made Lucas stop to take it all in. Whispering Oaks was a beautiful town—always had been—and it would always be his home.

They decided to celebrate the cast removal with a sushi platter and Japanese beer. Lucas was fairly amazed with how well his father worked the chopsticks.

"You know, Lucas," his dad said, stuffing a scallop roll into his mouth. He chased it down with a long draw on his beer. "I'm really looking forward to going back to school next year as an ordinary math teacher and an assistant coach."

"Wait. Are you saying Jocelyn got the position of head coach?"

"She didn't tell you?"

"We aren't exactly speaking." He dropped the portion of California roll he'd snagged between his chopsticks into the soy-and-wasabi sauce, then struggled to pick it back up.

His response got a suspicious stare from his dad. "Found out yesterday. You mean you two aren't even talking now?"

Lucas took a long drink. "Let's just say we've said everything we needed to say."

"You didn't break up with that girl, did you?" Kieran leaned forward on his elbows.

"Dad. We'd only gone out a few times. We weren't going together or anything."

"You know damn well that she's the kind of lady a man gets involved with. She isn't one of those superficial flighty things you find all over the place. She's solid. The kind of stuff you fall in love with."

Was the entire family conspiring against him? "And you know all of this, how?"

"I married a girl just like her. Your mother and I met in college and fell in love. She insisted we stay friends for a while first. When it was time to graduate we forgot we lived on opposite sides of the states. Guess who decided to move across the country to make her happy?" Kieran pointed to his chest with empty chopsticks.

Not wanting to meet his father's intense stare, suddenly the little green plate decoration got all of Lucas's attention.

"Hell, I've watched Jocelyn grow up, become a woman. She's what a man should look for in a wife."

"Then I hope she finds the right man." The surge of irritation, and the thought of actually losing Jocelyn, had him tearing his napkin in two.

Dad put his beer glass down. "You're a good man, Lucas. I wouldn't have made it through all these weeks without your help and your sister's before that. Your mother and I didn't raise dummies. I'm saying this because I know I used to ride you about slacking off, but you're a changed man, now. You've served your country. Matured. You know how to get things done. How to be a man. The only thing I'm not impressed with right now is you walking away from a good thing. The best thing."

Lucas pushed his plate away and pinched his lips tight rather than say anything disrespectful to his father like *Mind your own damn business, would you?*

"Are you done?" he asked as his dad finished the last of the sushi on the platter and his beer. "I'd like to spend some time this afternoon at the auto body shop."

"Sure," his dad said, digging for his wallet. "Since I gave all the advice, I guess I should pay, huh?"

"I won't argue with that."

"See? I told you, you're a wise man."

As they walked back to the car for the short drive home, his dad stopped. "If you haven't been talking to Jocelyn, then you probably don't know that she's due to receive the Teacher of the Year award next week at an assembly."

Lucas's head shot up. "Which day?" How cool was that? He knew she had what it took to be a good coach, and obviously she was a fantastic teacher. And now the students and her teacher peers were reinforcing that. A bubble of pride rose in his chest.

"Wednesday."

He got into the car and waited for his dad to do the same. "Can anyone come?"

"Of course."

They drove home in companionable silence. Lucas pulled into the driveway and dropped his father off, then checked his watch. Instead of going to the valley to the auto body shop like he said he would, he really headed north for his counseling appointment in Oxnard.

Chapter Twelve

Lucas sat at the computer in the home office Wednesday and fired off an email to Jake in North Carolina.

"I'm leaving. Are you coming?" His dad stood at the door dangling the car keys and looking irritated.

"Go ahead. You can drive yourself over. I'll meet you there," Lucas said, not looking up from the keyboard.

His father grunted and left. Down the hall Lucas heard him on the cell phone. "Hey, since I *can* drive myself, Bev, stand out front at school and I'll pick you up." A beat later Lucas heard, "I know, free at last!"

Truth was, his parents didn't need him around anymore. At this point, all he'd do was get in their way. After sending the first message, Lucas sent another email to David in the valley. He'd almost made his decision.

* * *

Jocelyn finished grading the last quiz while sitting at her desk. Because she was in the bungalow building she could keep her door open, have fresh air and sunshine and look outside instead of into the usual noisy hallways. She glanced up to see a shadow looming at the door. The dark silhouette leaned against the frame, and her heart dropped a beat…until she recognized sandy-blond hair. It was Jack Lightfoot, her fellow teacher and Anne Grady's fiancé.

"What's up?" she asked, putting her red pencil back in the holder and feeling a twinge of disappointment it was Jack instead of Lucas with a huge change of heart.

"You about ready?"

For what? And then she remembered. She'd been so bent on not thinking about losing Lucas, and failing miserably, she'd forgotten all about the assembly.

"Oh! What time is it?" She glanced at her watch and realized it was time to head over to the auditorium for the end-of-year awards assembly.

"It's past time. Let's go." Tall, tan, good-looking, the math teacher and part-time volunteer fireman pulled his hands out of his slacks pockets. "Come on, I'll walk you over."

She tidied her desk and locked the quizzes inside, grabbed her purse and scurried toward the door, locking it behind her. "I totally forgot."

"That you're getting the Teacher of the Year award? How'd you do that?"

The lantana bushes along the walkway flared with

bright fire-orange blooms, briefly distracting her. "I've had a lot on my mind lately."

"Taking over as head coach is a big responsibility."

"Yeah, that too."

Jack's piercing green eyes latched on to her evasive glance. "Something you want to talk about?"

"Nah. Since you're practically a relative, I don't want to drag you into my problems."

"Whose relative?"

"Lucas."

He stopped walking on the secluded path leading from the bungalows toward the grouping of larger buildings. An ancient oak tree in the center of the school shaded his face. "Talk to me."

"Oh, you don't want to hear my problems. It's just…"

"Getting a Grady to commit is like waiting for Congress to vote unanimously on a bill."

"Exactly!"

He gave her a thoughtful, knowing smile.

"How did you get Anne to come around?"

"You have to play dirty, Jocelyn. Twist an arm or two."

"But Lucas is bigger than me."

Jack slid her a tolerant glance. "I got Anne to come around by refusing to take no for an answer. By making sure she knew exactly how I felt about her. By pinning her in a corner and not letting her skip out until she gave me the answer I wanted to hear." He glanced over her shoulder, sidetracked in his own thoughts for a second. "I knew she loved me, but getting her to see it took some work."

Jocelyn sighed and started walking again. She'd told Lucas she loved him, and all he'd done was stare at the fireplace bricks. So much for laying the cards on the table. As of today, she was completely out of ideas. They approached the auditorium in silence, but just before they reached the backstage steps, Jack pulled her aside.

"Don't let him leave without facing you again. Make him tell you straight up he doesn't care about you. He can't, because he does. He'll crack. I guarantee."

She started to protest, the mere thought of getting her heart stomped on again made her stomach do a double backflip. "You know something I don't?"

"He's a guy, so he needs prodding. If you love him, go after him. That's what I did with Anne—not that she's a guy, just a stubborn Grady—and come September…well, you already know that story."

Jocelyn smiled remembering how miserable Jack was a few short months ago when he'd enlisted her into helping him get a date with Anne, as opposed to how happy he was these days. Engaged! His never-back-down technique had certainly paid off for him. Maybe it could for her, too? But how much more humiliation could her ego take?

"Come on, you guys. They've already started the awards ceremony." A student stagehand stood by the entrance. They skipped up the steps, and he rushed them toward the curtains, then urged Jocelyn to sit in the one remaining chair at the closest end of the stage.

The principal, Mrs. Saroyan, was already standing at the podium on a booster block. She was wearing her signature business suit, spike heels and all, and giving her opening remarks.

It was time to switch gears, put Lucas out of her mind and smile for the school and the students who'd voted her Teacher of the Year. She didn't necessarily feel as if she deserved this honor, but she needed to bask in the love from everyone giving her this award. She'd given teaching and coaching her best efforts this year, and it had paid off.

Too bad all of her efforts on Lucas's behalf at the up-close-and-personal level hadn't been as successful as her school year.

He hadn't called all week. She hadn't seen him since she'd told him she loved him. Well, she was through being his personal rah-rah, you-can-do-it cheerleader. It was time for Lucas to step up for himself. She couldn't force him into loving her, no matter how much she loved him. Now if she could just convince herself to give up hope.

She glanced down the row of chairs on the stage at Jack Lightfoot taking his seat on the other end. If only the Jack Lightfoot method for winning over the love of your life could work for her, too.

Across the stage, a long table was covered in trophies and certificates. This would be one long assembly. Jocelyn settled in, trying her best to keep her attention on Mrs. Saroyan.

* * *

Lucas combed his hair, patted on some aftershave and headed out the door for the Mustang. According to his watch, the assembly had already started. He didn't want to miss Jocelyn's big moment, so he pressed the speed limit on the way there. Five minutes later he rolled into a full parking lot and found a space way at the back. Sprinting toward the building he blew through the entry doors and slid across the foyer linoleum toward the auditorium entrance.

The room was packed and dark, and he didn't want to disrupt any of the ceremony, so he leaned against the back wall, soon finding Jocelyn on stage at the end of the front row. She looked pretty, as usual, with her hair down, and she wore a dress. He especially liked when she wore dresses. This one was dark blue with a short powder-blue sweater. He also liked watching her crossed leg nervously pump, waiting while the principal made introduction after introduction, handing out department trophies like free lunches. The shoe dangling off the end of Jocelyn's toes, as she pumped away, gave him pause.

Finally, they came to Teacher of the Year.

Mrs. Saroyan introduced his dad, who appeared from backstage and received a warm and exuberant welcome. Lucas hadn't expected him to be involved in the presentation. He sauntered across the stage like he owned the place, and when he got to the podium his dad lifted his left leg and right arm. "Look, no casts!"

That drew raucous applause. "Go, Coach!" And some razzing. "Finally!" and "Where's the Harley?"

It did make sense to have Dad present the award because he'd been the award's recipient several times in his career. He took the mic from Mrs. Saroyan and, when the applause died down, in his usual take-charge voice, he proceeded to explain why Jocelyn Howard deserved the award.

"Every year, the teachers and students receive an opportunity to nominate someone for teacher of the year. As teachers, we get to vote for deserving peers, and you students *finally* get your say." He waited and let the chuckles and sparse slow claps die down. "Over the years, I've noticed one quality that seems to prevail for every Teacher of the Year, and that quality is— the gift of encouragement. The teachers who win this award have tapped into the need for the human spirit to be bolstered and inspired. To be challenged, yet not just throwing someone into the pool, but jumping in with them, encouraging them through every stroke until they reach the other side.

"We have many students reaching toward goals they'd never dreamed of before because of this particular Teacher of the Year. She has a huge heart, solid skills as a science teacher and newfound talent as a track coach. She also helped raise a record amount at our sports department fund-raiser.

"I don't think there's anything any one of you could throw at Ms. Howard that she couldn't handle."

The students broke in with more applause.

Lucas glanced at Jocelyn, whose leg had gone completely still, and, even from this distance, he could tell she was tearing up because he knew her better than anyone. After all, he'd known her all his life.

"Ms. Howard, because of you, students will be going to college who never dreamed they had a chance. You've inoculated our student body with your genuine love of anatomy and physiology. You've soothed students with your naturally cheerful attitude. Several of our athletes will have an opportunity to impress university coaches at the upcoming state track finals, thanks to your stepping up when Whispering Oaks High needed you." He paused to share his winning Coach Grady smile. "I can't think of anyone I'd rather give this award to."

His dad turned back to the audience. "Let's give Ms. Howard a big hand."

The auditorium overflowed with applause and Lucas joined in. He'd never felt more proud of anyone in his life. Jocelyn deserved all the kudos. There was no one in the world like her.

So why was he planning to leave her?

Jocelyn stood. It wasn't as if she hadn't spoken in front of hundreds of students before, but this felt different. Wishing she wasn't so nervous, she gathered her composure and walked slowly to meet Coach Grady. He smiled widely and genuinely, and instead of accepting the oak tree–shaped trophy, she hugged him. Though seemingly unprepared for that, he hugged her back. She glanced into his moist blue eyes and imagined she saw the same wish there she had for herself—that Lucas would come to his senses and figure out she was the best damn woman on earth for him. But she'd probably read into Coach Grady's encouraging and kind gaze.

Taking the trophy, she stepped up to the podium and, not trusting her hands with trembling, waited while Kieran replaced the microphone in the holder. The applause continued, and it warmed her heart as she scanned the audience through her blurry eyes.

"Could we turn up the lights a little bit?" she asked while she unfolded some notes she'd quickly jotted down earlier that morning. "I'd like to see everybody." After a quick response from the stage crew the room was illuminated. She took a moment to savor all the smiling faces as she continued to scan the crowd. Far at the back she glimpsed a man. She'd recognize that build anywhere, but not expecting him today, she squinted to make out his features. To make sure she wasn't imagining what she longed to see more than anything. Him.

It was Lucas, the man she loved, and he was leaning against the wall, arms crossed, waiting for her to speak along with everyone else. Her pulse did a high jump, thumping in her chest. Lucas hadn't left without saying goodbye after all. With her heart palpitating with hope, she had a speech to make, and it required her full concentration. Knowing he was here made her even more nervous.

"Thank you." She'd spoken too close to the microphone and there was ringing feedback. "Sorry." She adjusted her distance, regretting beginning her speech with an apology. "After those amazing words from Coach Grady, I don't know how I can possibly live up to this honor. I guess the best thing I can do is be honest with all of you." She glanced to the back of the auditorium again, making sure Lucas was still there and deciding to speak from her heart.

"To the students, let me say that you've gotten this far in life and have learned a few things, with or without my input. But I've still got something important to tell you. I hope you'll agree when I say, as your teacher and coach, there is nothing more enabling than team spirit. Team spirit is a disease we all need to catch because it gives us strength we couldn't possibly create on our own.

"Aristotle said the whole is greater than the sum of its parts. The reason for this, I believe, is because of synergy. It's what happens when everyone works together for a specific goal. Each person brings something special to the group, and what adds up on an individual-by-individual basis becomes much, much more. One person's energy together with ten other people becomes an explosion of force. In other words—team spirit rocks!"

The students must have liked her analogy because the room rocked with applause. Her nerves settled a bit, and she had more to share, something she hoped would hit home, especially with Lucas.

"Something I've learned over my life is the importance of sticking things out when life gets tough. For instance, Coach Grady recently totaled his Harley and faced the biggest challenge in his life. Now, next semester, he'll be back and ready to pick up where he left off." The students whistled and stomped, obviously happy to have their old teacher and coach return. She glanced at him—and he had a question in his eyes. "Maybe not exactly where he left off, but he's open to change because that's what life is all about. Right, Coach?" He nodded with a smile stretching his cheeks. "We have to be flexible in life.

"Recently, when I found myself taking over as track coach and heading up the annual athletic fund-raiser, I completely doubted myself." She cleared her throat, thinking of how instrumental Lucas had been in her developing confidence as a leader, and suddenly she was overwhelmed with gratitude for him. He'd changed her life by encouraging her to apply for the new position. If only he'd give her a chance to tell him how important his faith in her had been before he ran off back east. "That's where team spirit came in for me, too. A friend of mine wouldn't let me quit or give up. I tried to bring my past into my present situation, and he wouldn't let me use it as an excuse." She glanced to the back of the auditorium to make sure he still hadn't left. He hadn't moved an inch, and stood intently listening.

"I promised to be honest with you all today, so I'm going to tell you that I've failed plenty in life. I graduated from high school with a free ride to college on a track scholarship, and I was on top of the world. Soon, reality kicked in, and hard work didn't seem enough to get me through. I couldn't do it all. I either had to be training all the time to stay in the top hurdling ranks, or working part-time for extra money, or cracking the books to pass the hours of classes I attended each day. Turns out I couldn't do it all and excel at anything, and eventually my grades and my track performance suffered. I lost my scholarship. So when this opportunity to take over the track team came up, I didn't feel worthy to step into Coach Grady's shoes." She hooked some hair behind her ear, searching for the best way to phrase it. "Well, this friend of mine, he convinced me I had a lot to offer. He told me I could work wonders if I believed in myself.

"What I'm getting at is we're all in this together. We need to share our burdens just as much as we share our joy. We need to support and comfort one another because that's what life is all about—being there for each other. Team spirit. Encouraging and sharing. I guess that's why you gave me this Teacher of the Year award, and I want to thank you for noticing that I care." She stopped to catch her breath as more applause broke out. "Let me leave you with one last thought. Each and every one of you needs to care, too. Life is a lot easier when we all work as a team. Thank you for being on my team. Thank you for letting me be a part of yours."

Jocelyn's sincere message rang true to Lucas. She'd spoken completely from her heart and in the process had reached inside his. He was running away from home again because life had gotten tough, and guess what, life would always be tough. It was the nature of the beast.

How long could he keep running from himself and the people who loved him and wanted the best for him?

He shot off a quick text message to Jake: Change in plans. Will call later. Then another to David: Want to take you up on that offer. Pocketing his cell phone, he saw the students jump to their feet, and if he hadn't already been standing he would have, too. His hands hurt from clapping so hard. Hell, he even whistled as he moved toward the stage. He was so damn proud of Joss.

He watched Jocelyn being inundated with outstretched hands wanting to shake hers. She high-fived with a dozen students as more gathered in line to congratulate her.

How could he leave behind the best part of his life—the girl next door, his family and Whispering Oaks?

He finally got it. She'd love him whether he was a student or a professional. She'd love him on the journey there—not just when he'd reached his goal. The term slacker didn't exist in her vocabulary. He didn't need to slink away until he felt worthy of her; she loved him right here, right now, just the way he was.

Weaving through the crowd, he drew closer and caught hold of Jocelyn's tear-filled gaze, offering her a rueful smile in exchange. He wasn't as dense as she thought he was. He had a surprise or two left in his arsenal. Because she was the perfect person to be with and love…*to hell with this nonchalant walk-toward-the-stage business.*

He jogged toward her around a clump of kids, and

she reached out for him. He grabbed her hands as she leaned over. Way over. They kissed briefly. He grabbed her by the waist and lifted her off the stage, down where he could kiss her the way he wanted.

Their lips came together in a heated surge, as if they hadn't seen each other in years. He kissed like a guy who had no intention of ever leaving town. Because he wasn't going to. He'd finally manned up and changed his plans. Starting now.

Savoring her lips pressed tightly to his, his nerve endings tingling to full attention, the sudden awareness of hooting and cheers reminded him they weren't alone.

A goofy chant started, "Kiss her. Kiss her," accentuated by clapping hands picking up tempo with each chant.

He smiled over her lips, knowing her ears and face were probably beet red from all the attention. He broke away, pressing his forehead to hers. "Let's skip this joint."

Disappointment wiped away her smile. "I've got one more class this afternoon."

Lucas swung around to find his parents standing nearby, looking on and grinning. Seeing his mother reminded him about the quote she'd recited to him the other morning. Something about how the deepest love grows from friendship. She was right.

"I'll cover for you." His father's voice broke into their private world.

"You will?" Jocelyn asked, still locked tightly in Lucas's embrace. He didn't plan to let go of her for hours to come.

There was no point in hiding his feelings for Jocelyn from his parents, who already knew what true love was. They'd been on to him before he'd even figured out how he felt, yet they had given him enough space to work through it by himself.

"I'm still qualified," his dad said. "I'll do what any substitute worth their salt does—I'll babysit. Just tell me which room and what to do and…"

"You can hand out the quizzes and collect homework. How's that?"

"I can handle that. I'll even take attendance." His grin was contagious.

Mrs. Saroyan was nearby; Lucas hadn't noticed her but even she gave a smile and an approving tip of her bouffant hairdo. Jocelyn dug into her sweater pocket for a key, then tossed it to his dad.

"Good. Now that we've settled that," Lucas said, "I've got a mint Mustang in the parking lot ready to whisk you away."

She leaned into him and rested her head on his shoulder. "I can't wait."

For good measure and to rally the troops again, he laid one more big hungry kiss on her mouth.

The students didn't let him down.

Lucas parked the car at what had become his favorite lookout point over Whispering Oaks. The sun was high in the sky, a crop of sunflowers seemed to smile at them from across the lot and the fresh scent of cut grass from the local park at the base of the ridge wafted up to his nose. The girl he loved snuggled against his shoulder as they looked out at their hometown.

"So, are you sure you don't mind being involved with a guy who's starting at the bottom, a guy who finally has a vision for his life but will take several years to achieve it?"

Her head popped up from his chest. "Yes, but what are you talking about?"

"If I'm going to school, I can't just live off my parents, and the GI bill will only cover so much, so I'm starting a new job."

"Wait. Slow down. Last I heard you were leaving town to go to school. What's changed?"

He kissed her slowly with all the love he felt. "You. And the fact I have an offer to start work with David at the auto body shop."

She squealed.

"He restores classic cars on the side, and he's willing to pay me to work on a few he has lined up while I'm taking my basic education courses for the PA program at Marshfield Community College."

"But I thought you were interested in sports medicine?"

"It's interesting, but it didn't click for me. Then I found out about the physician's assistant program, and it seemed to suit my skills as a medic better."

"That's fantastic!"

"You won't be embarrassed having a grease monkey, junior college dude as a boyfriend?"

"Not on your life." She kissed his chin. "You always look so sexy leaning over the car engine, wearing those tight jeans and showing off your tattoos with your shirt off."

He squeezed her tighter. "You're going to get yourself in trouble if you keep talking like that."

"That's my goal."

He held her face and kissed her tenderly—savoring the mouth he hoped to spend the rest of his life kissing.

She broke away, her brows pinched together. "What about your friend in Raleigh? And school back there?"

"Jake will be fine with my decision. We'll keep in touch. Check in with each other to make sure we're both doing okay. Did I mention he has PTSD, too?"

"No. You didn't discuss any of your plans with Jake with me. Remember?" she said with somber eyes.

"I do, and I'm sorry. From now on, you'll be the first person I talk to about any big decisions."

She sighed. "Really?"

"Definitely. You're the most important person in the world to me." He'd been honest and now he'd made her cry. "Aw, come on, this is supposed to be a happy day."

"These are tears of joy." She wiped at the corners of her eyes.

He kissed her wet and salty cheeks one at a time. "So

is that a yes that you'll stick by my side while I work out all the particulars?"

Beaming through her tears she didn't miss a beat. "Lucas Grady, that's the only place I've ever wanted to be."

* * * * *

COMING NEXT MONTH
from Harlequin® Special Edition®
AVAILABLE JULY 23, 2013

#2275 THE MAVERICK'S SUMMER LOVE
Montana Mavericks: Rust Creek Cowboys
Christyne Butler
Handsome carpenter Dean Pritchett comes to Rust Creek Falls, Montana, to help repair flood damage. But can single mom Shelby, who has a checkered past, fix Dean's wounded heart?

#2276 IT'S A BOY!
The Camdens of Colorado
Victoria Pade
Widow Heddy Hanrahan is about to give up her bakery when struggling single dad Lang Camden comes to her rescue. Can Heddy overcome her past to find love with her knight in a shining apron?

#2277 WANTED: A REAL FAMILY
The Mommy Club
Karen Rose Smith
When physical therapist Sara Stevens's home burns down, her ex-patient Jase invites Sara and her daughter to live near him. But when sparks of a personal nature ignite, Sara wonders if she's made a mistake....

#2278 HIS LONG-LOST FAMILY
Those Engaging Garretts!
Brenda Harlen
When Kelly Cooper returned to Pinehurst, New York, she wanted her daughter, Ava, to know her father—not to rekindle a romance with Jackson Garrett. But sometimes first love deserves a second chance....

#2279 HALEY'S MOUNTAIN MAN
The Colorado Fosters
Tracy Madison
Outsider Gavin Daugherty isn't looking for companionship, so he's taken aback when Steamboat Springs, Colorado, sweetheart Haley Foster befriends him. When their friendship blossoms into something more, will Gavin run for the hills?

#2280 DATE WITH DESTINY
Helen Lacey
Grace Preston moved away from Crystal Point, Australia, after school, leaving her family—and heartbroken boyfriend, Cameron—behind. When a troubled Grace returns home, she finds that some loves just can't remain in the past....

You can find more information on upcoming Harlequin® titles, free excerpts and more at www.Harlequin.com.

HSECNM0713

Handsome carpenter Dean Pritchett comes to Rust Creek Falls to help rebuild the town after the Great Montana Flood and meets a younger woman with a checkered past. Can Shelby Jenkins repair the damage to this cowboy's heart?

***

Shelby laid a hand on his arm. "Please, don't stop. I like listening to you."

"Yeah?"

She nodded, trying to erase the tingling sensation that danced from her palm to her elbow thanks to the warmth of his skin.

"My brothers and I have worked on projects together, but usually it's just me and whatever piece of furniture I'm working on."

"Solitary sounds good to me. My job is nothing but working with people. Sometimes that can be hard, too."

"Especially when those people aren't so nice?"

Shelby nodded, wrapping her arms around her bent knees as she stared out at the nearby creek.

Dean leaned closer, brushing back the hair that had fallen against her cheek, his thumb staying behind to move back and forth across her cheek.

Her breath caught, then vanished completely the moment he touched her. She was frozen in place, her arms locked around her knees, held captive by the simple press of his thumb.

He gently lifted her head while lowering his. The warmth of

his breath floated across her skin, his green eyes darkening to a deep jade as he looked down at her.

Before their lips could meet, Shelby broke free.

Dropping her chin, she kept her gaze focused on the sliver of blanket between them as heat blazed across her cheeks.

Dean stilled for a moment, then eased away. "Okay. This is a bit awkward."

"I'm sorry." She closed her eyes, not wanting to see the disappointment, or worse, in his eyes as the apology rushed past her lips. "I haven't— It's been a long time since I've—"

"It's okay, Shelby. No worries. I'll wait."

She looked up and found nothing in his gaze but tenderness mixed with banked desire. "You will? Why?"

"Because when the time is right, kissing you is going to be so worth it."

***

We hope you enjoyed this sneak peek at
USA TODAY *bestselling author Christyne Butler's*
new Harlequin® Special Edition® book,
THE MAVERICK'S SUMMER LOVE,
the next installment in
MONTANA MAVERICKS:
RUST CREEK COWBOYS,
a brand-new six-book continuity
launching in July 2013!

SADDLE UP AND READ 'EM!

Looking for another great Western read? Check out these August reads from the HOME & FAMILY category!

THE LONG, HOT TEXAS SUMMER by Cathy Gillen Thacker
McCabe Homecoming
Harlequin American Romance

HOME TO THE COWBOY by Amanda Renee
Harlequin American Romance

HIS FOREVER VALENTINE by Marie Ferrarella
Forever, Texas
Harlequin American Romance

THE MAVERICK'S SUMMER LOVE by Christyne Butler
Montana Mavericks
Harlequin Special Edition

*Look for these great Western reads AND MORE
available wherever books are sold or visit*
www.Harlequin.com/Westerns